Home
for
Winter

OTHER TITLES BY REBECCA BOXALL

Christmas at the Vicarage

REBECCA BOXALL

Home
for
Winter

LAKE UNION
PUBLISHING

Published by Lake Union Publishing, Seattle

www.apub.com

Amazon, the Amazon logo, and Lake Union Publishing are trademarks of Amazon.com, Inc., or its affiliates.

ISBN-13: 9781503940055
ISBN-10: 1503940055

Cover design © blacksheep-uk.com

Printed in the United States of America

In memory of Connie Crouch (1895–1917)
And for Dan

And the Lord said unto Cain, where is Abel thy brother?
And he said, I know not: am I my brother's keeper?
Genesis 4:9

PART ONE

1.
FEBRUARY 2015

It was the thick of winter when Serena and Will moved into the Vicarage. A cold, damp day in February. The electricity wasn't working and as they moved carefully around the enormous old house, trying to locate the trip switch, Serena thought she'd never felt as cold in her life.

They'd viewed the house when it was full of the warmth and clutter of a large family, but now the Vicarage seemed chill and stark. Even once the electricity had been turned on, the ceiling lights did little to brighten the house.

'Lamps will transform the place,' Serena said bravely and Will put an arm around her.

'We'll get it sorted in no time,' he said. 'A fresh start,' he added, and Serena smiled, although the smile, like her laughter nowadays, no longer seemed to rise from deep within her. Both were, while not false, more habitual than anything else.

It had been almost six months now and Will was keen for them to move on with their lives. Serena was too, although she was relying on Will's energy and enthusiasm to drive their fresh start forward. He was the one who'd spotted the advert for the post as vicar of Cattlebridge in East Sussex, thinking it might be time to flee London and enjoy the benefits of rural life.

Their new village was only half an hour's drive from where Serena had grown up, close to the coastal town of Rye, and was quintessentially English. The Vicarage faced onto a street lined with beautiful, historic houses and was situated next door to the Norman church, its back garden leading through to the graveyard.

Next to the church stood the Black Horse pub, and a little further along the lane was the high street, where a number of ancient cottages and a selection of useful shops could be found – a grocer's, newsagent's, chemist's, butcher's and hairdresser's, as well as a florist's, bakery and gift shop. Past all of these was a quaint bookshop, and beside this was a store Serena was eager to explore, resembling an Aladdin's Cave full of antiques, pine and other treasures.

That first morning, Serena had nipped to the newsagent's to buy a pint of milk and a paper while they waited for the removal vans to arrive and she'd been intrigued to hear the proprietor and a couple of locals discussing some kind of local mystery.

'Do you think they've heard about the place being cursed?' the woman behind the till had asked. But as they all clocked Serena, the chatter had stopped abruptly, making her wonder if they'd been talking about the Vicarage. She sincerely hoped not.

'Colonel Feltham-Jones!' one of the customers bellowed at Serena immediately, introducing himself. He was lanky, with only one arm and rather battered-looking spectacles. He seemed kindly though, despite his brisk military diction.

'Serena Meadows,' she smiled, offering her hand. Fortunately, it was the left arm the Colonel was missing, so their handshake wasn't too awkward. Serena introduced herself to the rest of the group and everyone seemed friendly enough, though she knew they'd instantly begin to analyse her as soon as she stepped foot over the threshold.

Village life. Serena was no stranger to the countryside and she'd been quite content to go along with Will's plans to move to Cattlebridge. It was just that she hadn't been able – not yet, anyway – to throw herself into them.

But a move required some energy at least, and Serena was interested enough to explore the house. She could barely remember visiting the month before, so while Will directed the removal men as to where their carefully labelled boxes should be deposited, Serena gave herself a guided tour of her new home – a gothic Victorian pile that really couldn't have been more of a contrast to the modern bungalow they'd lived in last.

She began by retracing her steps to the grand entrance hall, which housed a huge fireplace and, currently, little else. A staircase swept up from the hall, but for now Serena remained on the ground floor. To the right of the front door was a room that Mrs Pipe, the housekeeper they'd somehow acquired with the Vicarage, called the library, though Will had decided to use it as a study. Mrs Pipe was actually employed as full-time housekeeper for the occupants of an ostentatious house nearby – the Smythes – but had always spent a couple of hours a week at the Vicarage, assisting the incumbent vicar with the upkeep of the place. She was a real character, with a charming Sussex accent and a vocabulary full of provincialisms, although she wasn't quite the cosy housekeeper Serena might have hoped for, with an unsmiling face, steely grey hair and hooded eyes. She was more than a little unnerving.

The study was one of the cosier rooms in the house, with a fireplace, plentiful bookshelving and large sash windows looking out onto the street at the front of the building. Serena and Will's squishy cream sofas had just been placed on either side of the hearth, while small side tables, Will's desk and a colourful rug helped create a homely atmosphere.

Across the hall was the drawing room. In here, an enormous chandelier hung from the corniced ceiling over an area that cried out for smart sofas and a coffee table. The room was bright, with windows to the front of the house and several more along the west wall, offering a view of the garden beyond. Aside from the chandelier and some rather riotous floral wallpaper, the space stood empty.

Standing there, contemplating, Serena heard footsteps and turned around.

'You okay?' Will asked. He came to stand behind her, wrapping his arms round her shoulders. Serena leant her head back against his chest.

'Just wondering how on earth we're going to fill the house with furniture. The vicarage in London was half the size of this place.'

'At least!' laughed Will. 'But I know you and your love of second-hand bargains. It won't take you long. It'll be a project, just until you're ready to start work again.'

'Yes,' Serena agreed. 'Just what I need. Will, I think one of the chaps is after you,' she said, spotting a removal man hovering nearby.

Serena watched the two of them disappear, then continued with her inspection, past the wood-panelled dining room and down the stairs to the basement.

Here, Serena felt most at home – although the kitchen was rather old and crumbling, the pale blue Rayburn was warm and cosy, lending a comforting glow to the room as well as serving as a cooker.

Beside the stove, their own pine table and chairs had been arranged on one side, while on the other was a wall-mounted butler sink with blue and white Victorian tiles above and a teak draining board to the side. There was also a vast built-in dresser, though the item that really dominated the room was a central work table, also made of teak and with numerous drawers under the worktop, presumably for storing cutlery and other items. Serena thought it must have been around since the house had been built.

Serena loved all the little rooms that branched off from the main kitchen. Mrs Pipe had run her through their uses earlier in the day.

'This be the laundry and right here's the scullery. Used to be the overflow kitchen back in Victorian times. That's why there be two sinks, so some poor maid could wash the dishes in here without so much as a window to look out of.'

There was also a walk-in larder and, Mrs Pipe had explained, a butler's pantry, outside which hung a charming set of bells with signs beneath them indicating which room in the house was requiring servants' services – another relic from Victorian times.

Serena was amazed at how little the Vicarage seemed to have been updated over the years, but then the diocese was always stretched and rarely provided the resident vicar with funds for anything other than necessary plumbing and electric work or, at a push, some re-roofing. Will and Serena had decided to take out a loan and stump up themselves to make the Vicarage more habitable.

Working her way back up the stairs, Serena bumped into Will, who planted a quick kiss on her lips before chasing down the stairs after a removal man who was about to deposit boxes of books in the kitchen rather than the study. Serena smiled briefly to herself. Will was incredibly organised, a trait that appealed to her almost as much as his enthusiasm.

Negotiating another man bearing a heavy box, she wove her way up the sweeping staircase to the first-floor landing, brushing her hand along the banister as she climbed. On this floor, there were several bedrooms, including a magnificent master with a modern en suite and even a dressing room. There was also a nursery, with a beautiful mural on one wall, which stabbed at Serena's heart. She closed the door quickly then gasped as she came upon Mrs Pipe standing silently on the landing, a grim expression on her face.

'Give you a fright, did I?'

'Sorry, it's just . . . the room. The nursery.' Serena couldn't explain it, but her heart was pounding.

'No need for you to be going in that room, is there? You want to stay out of there.'

'Why?' Serena asked, but Mrs Pipe had turned and disappeared down the stairs.

Confused and a little rattled, Serena warily pushed open the next door along and found a spacious family bathroom where a cast-iron roll-top bath stood resplendent on black and white tiles. Catching sight of herself in the mirror above the washbasin, she stepped closer to consider the face peering back at her.

She was blonde, ringlets springing from her head in the wild fashion they had since she was a young child, and her eyes were green with silver flecks. Surprisingly, her eyebrows were thick and dark – a dramatic contrast to her blonde hair. She and Luna had tried bleaching them once, when they were about fifteen, but they'd both looked so odd. Their faces had seemed too round and pale without the brows to add definition. Now Serena decided they needed a pluck, but other than that she thought she looked alright. A little tired, perhaps, but not so unlike her old self. Appearances could be deceptive, she mused. She sighed and turned from the room, continuing to the bedroom next door.

Serena climbed at last to the attic rooms, the old servants' quarters. She shivered, wrapping her thick cardigan around herself more tightly as she gazed out onto the desolate garden below, listening to the windows rattle disconcertingly in their frames.

She wondered if she would ever feel like herself again.

2.
DECEMBER 1989

Being an identical twin was both a blessing and a curse. It had its advantages – a ready-made best friend for one – and it was impossible to feel lonely. Tricks could always be played on friends, family and, best of all, teachers. But it was hard to establish any sort of identity when most of the time nobody dared address you by name in case they had the wrong twin. And everyone always assumed you both had the same character, just because you looked the same, when in the case of Serena and Luna this couldn't have been further from the truth.

Serena first realised quite how different she was from her twin two weeks before Christmas in 1989. They were nine. An excitable Luna disturbed Serena, who was playing with her dolls, and dragged her through to their parents' room.

'Guess what I've found in Mum's wardrobe?' she whispered.

'What?' Serena asked.

'Our Christmas presents!'

'Are they wrapped?'

'Yes, but I can easily sneak a look inside the wrapping. Do you want to know what you've got?' Luna asked, pulling out a present labelled with Serena's name.

'No!' Serena replied, adamant. 'I want it to be a surprise.'

'It's that Barbie car you wanted!' Luna exclaimed, not listening, abuzz with the illicit nature of it all. 'The silver one without a roof! My turn now,' she said, arm back in the wardrobe, rummaging around, and Serena sat on her parents' bed miserably as each and every surprise was ruined.

On Christmas morning, Luna put on a display of wonder and gratitude that made Serena feel ill, while she couldn't help looking underwhelmed by her presents even though she'd wanted them desperately.

'You did want the Barbie Golf, didn't you, darling?' asked her father, later when they were alone. Serena felt tears spring to her eyes.

'Yes, Dad,' she said, nodding fiercely, but she knew she'd looked ungrateful and there was nothing she could do about it now.

It was the worst Christmas ever, compounded by an incident the day after Boxing Day. Returning from the pantomime, Serena couldn't find her new doll, a treasured gift from her maternal grandmother. Serena was mad about dolls in general, but this one was truly special, with her long dark hair, porcelain skin and blinking eyelids. She knew she'd left the doll on top of her bed, but arriving home it was no longer there.

'Have you seen my doll?' she asked Luna. 'Elizabeth?' She'd given the doll the kind of dignified name it deserved. Luna stopped spinning around their bedroom. She loved watching how her skirt spun round and round.

'No,' she replied. 'Serena, don't tell me you've lost that beautiful dolly. Granny will be so upset.'

'I haven't lost her,' said Serena, messing up their room in her desperation to find her. 'I left her right here,' she explained, pointing at the bedcovers. Before long, the entire family was searching the house for Elizabeth.

'You didn't have it . . . her . . . at the pantomime and leave her there, did you?' asked her father, but by now Serena was in floods of panicked tears. She felt sick at how thoughtlessly she'd managed to lose her precious doll. Serena had been certain she'd left Elizabeth on her bed, but she was doubting herself now. Eventually, she fell asleep, her tears finally drying.

The next morning, she pulled herself up and blearily turned on the bedside light, looking over to see if Luna was awake yet. And there, snuggled up beside her sister, was Elizabeth.

Luna lay sleeping, her face the picture of innocence.

3.

FEBRUARY 2015

Will always slept the sleep of the dead so when the doorbell rang in the middle of the night, it was Serena, the lightest of sleepers, who padded downstairs in her dressing gown with a golf club for protection. She warily opened the heavy front door and was shocked to find, standing on the doorstep and soaked through with rain, the most beautiful young woman she'd ever seen – she had exceptionally long hair, clear skin and a narrow nose from which a tiny jewel sparkled. Most striking of all, though, were her eyebrows: slim, dark and arched, they accentuated her oval face perfectly.

'I'm so sorry . . . disturbing you in the middle of the night. I just didn't know what to do, where to go . . . I'm running away from home,' the stranger gabbled.

'Come in, out of the rain!' Serena said and the girl flung herself into Serena's arms, sobbing.

'I'm sorry . . . It's so late . . .' she apologised again, stepping back.

'Don't even think about it,' Serena soothed. 'Now, let's get you sorted out.'

She was not unused to events such as this – a vicarage was quite frequently a port of call for the lost, the hungry and the grieving, most often in the middle of the night, and she wasn't bothered about being disturbed. She liked being able to help those in trouble, and the vicarage in London had often been a temporary shelter to various waifs and strays. Nowadays she could identify with them even more. Seeing the lost and desperate look in the girl's eyes was in some ways like looking into a mirror.

Practicalities had to be dealt with first. Serena led the girl upstairs to the family bathroom, where she began running a hot bath. She rooted around in a removal box that had been dumped in the airing cupboard, then handed her unexpected guest a large towel and a flannel.

'Have a nice bath to warm up,' Serena said. 'And while you're doing that, I'll find you something dry to wear.'

She shut the door and crept through the master bedroom to the dressing room where she located jeans, a T-shirt and a warm jumper, as well as thick socks.

'Clothes are just outside,' she called through to the bathroom before waiting patiently for the girl to emerge. 'I'm Serena, by the way!' she added. 'Just shout if you need me!'

Half an hour later, the two women were sitting with steaming mugs of tea, huddled as close to the Rayburn as possible.

'What happened?' asked Serena, gently curious.

'I had to leave . . .' the girl explained. Her sobs had abated, but her breath was still uneven and juddering. 'I was about to marry this guy. My father organised it. But he's so awful – he makes out he's this amazing, charming businessman, but on the rare occasions we're alone, he hits me. Only in certain places, so the bruises are never visible. There's this glint in his eye, a glimmer of anticipation. Not for the wedding, or our being together, but for the harm he'll be able to cause me once we're properly alone. I had to escape.'

'An arranged marriage?' asked Serena.

'A forced marriage in my case,' the stranger explained. 'I'm not at all against arranged marriages. A few of my friends have had really successful ones. But my father can be blind and he's been bowled over by this man's wealth and success and is determined I should marry him, regardless of what I think or feel. I'm sorry. I can't even say his name. He repulses me.'

'But couldn't you just tell your parents what he's really like? Surely they want you to be safe and happy?'

'My mother, yes, but she's completely in my father's shadow. My father and brother, they know I don't want to marry him, but they don't care. They will honestly kill me if they find me . . .' She tailed off, her dark eyes wide with fear.

'You'll have to forgive my ignorance, but are these kinds of marriages influenced by religion or culture?'

'Culture. Well, money and culture. My parents aren't even devout. But, in the small region in India my parents are from, it's the way things have always been done. The shame I'll have brought on the family now by running away . . .'

'They won't find you here,' Serena assured her. 'But where's your stuff? Is this bag all you have? How did you even get here? And what's your name? I'm sorry – too many questions.'

'That's alright, I understand. I'm Ashna,' the girl replied sadly. 'This evening I knew the time had come to leave. I couldn't stay any longer, with the wedding day edging closer. I packed a few things and, once I was certain my family were asleep, I made my escape. I live in Essex and I literally didn't know where to go, especially as I don't have any money. I just thought I'd hitch and see where I ended up. Probably stupidly dangerous, but I was that desperate. I just thought if I could make it to the countryside, at least an hour from home, that might be a start . . . But if my father and brother find me, they'll kill me,' Ashna repeated, the dark pools of her eyes glistening with new tears. She was still shivering and Serena rummaged around in the laundry, where she managed to locate a warm blanket in a removal box marked *Bedding*. She returned to the kitchen and wrapped it round Ashna's thin shoulders.

'Will they have any idea where you've gone?' asked Serena.

Ashna shook her head. 'We have no connections to this place. I only ended up here because one of the guys I managed to hitch a ride with was on his way home to the village after a shift at the local hospital. I was upset and said I didn't know where to go, so he suggested I try the Vicarage. Dr Charles, he was called; he was so kind. He gave me his number in case I didn't have any luck here. Do you know him?'

'No,' said Serena with a smile. 'We only moved in today,' she explained. 'My partner, Will, is the new vicar. We hardly know anyone. In fact, you've arrived in the nick of time. You'll be company for me. You must stay as long as you need to. We have acres of space.'

'But I have no money,' Ashna lamented. 'How can I stay without paying for bed and board?'

Serena thought for a moment. It was clear Ashna was proud and reluctant to accept charity. 'Have you seen the state of the house?' she asked, looking around. Ashna's round eyes took in the ancient kitchen. 'The place is in dire need of a makeover,' Serena continued. 'Will's going to be busy with his new parish and I'm in no state to set about the renovation on my own.' She decided not to elaborate on the reason for this just now.

'Will you help me give the Vicarage a facelift, in return for bed and board?' she asked. Ashna reached out to take her hand and Serena gripped it, astonished at how smooth her skin was. The girl must be so young.

'How old are you?' Serena asked.

'Twenty-one,' Ashna replied. 'Serena, you're my saviour,' she added, and the deal was done.

4.
APRIL 1990

It was Miss Jones, their teacher at the local primary school, who seemed to be the only person to recognise that it was always Luna who made friends and Serena who was included by default. Luna was hugely popular, being one of those people whose dominant character draws others towards them. She was funny too, in a vicious sort of way, always devising hilarious nicknames for the teachers. She was responsible for the entire school calling the head teacher, the unfortunately named Mr Longbottom, 'Droopy Bum'.

Serena had once thought it would be nice to have a friend who was just hers and had made a special effort to befriend, as surreptitiously as she could, Louise Bradbury, who was new to the school in September the previous year.

An opportunity had arisen when the class were rehearsing for their nativity play in December. Luna had persuaded the teacher to give her the coveted role of Mary, while Serena was a snowflake with three other girls, including Louise. They'd been required to learn a special song and dance, which meant a separate rehearsal time to Luna, and it gave Serena the opportunity to chat and giggle with Louise before and after practice (and sometimes during, much to the music teacher's chagrin).

By the time of the Christmas party (the day after the nativity play), they were firm friends and instantly sat together in the hall while the teachers brought through all the sandwiches, cakes and jugs of squash. But, of course, Luna was also at the party and she quickly caught on that Serena had quietly made herself a friend. By the end of the autumn term, she'd managed to muscle in, charming Louise and turning things from duo to trio. Serena, resigned, had accepted the situation.

Now it was April.

'Serena Meadows, will you stay behind after class for a moment, please?' asked Miss Jones. Luna reluctantly left the classroom with the rest of the group, her large green eyes inquisitive.

'I have a favour to ask,' said Miss Jones. 'I thought about all the children in the class I might ask and decided you would be perfect for the job.' She smiled and Serena, feeling honoured, smiled back.

'What is it, Miss?' she asked.

'I have a nephew who's just started boarding school and, not only is he new to the school, but he's new to the country as well. His parents live on a Spanish island called Majorca and he's always gone to school there until now, but as he's just turned eleven – a little older than you – his parents have decided to send him to England for the rest of his education. I know he's feeling very lonely. He doesn't know anyone here and it's always awful starting a school midway through the year, when everyone else has already buddied up. I wondered whether you would write to him, as a pen pal? You have the best writing in the class and you're such a kind girl. I know you'll be able to cheer him up. What do you say?' asked Miss Jones, pushing her red spectacles further up her nose. Miss Jones was the best teacher Serena had ever had. She was young and glamorous and wore marvellously wacky clothes.

'But will he want to get letters from a girl?' asked Serena. The boys she knew weren't interested in girls at all.

'Ah, well, Freddie is very used to girls – he has three sisters. I think he'd love it.'

So Serena agreed, not realising at all that Miss Jones had Serena's interests at heart just as much as her nephew's. Serena was about to leave the classroom when she turned around.

'Should Luna write to him as well, Miss?' she asked.

Miss Jones shook her head firmly.

'No, Serena. Freddie can be just *your* friend,' she said, and Serena almost skipped out of the room. At last, she would have a friend of her own.

5.
FEBRUARY 2015

Will was concentrating, trying to prepare his sermon for the next day. It was his first morning service and he was anxious to make a good impression. Sermons were the making or breaking of a vicar, of that he was certain. They needed to be long enough to satisfy the die-hard churchgoers and short enough to avoid blank stares of boredom from the less devoted flock. Five minutes was about right in his view. Then they had to be amusing without being too flippant, and informative without being too know-it-all. It was one of the toughest parts of the job getting the balance right, week after week, and Mrs Pipe had already made her feelings on the subject clear.

'Not going to be one of those long-winded ones are you, Reverend Blacksmith?' she'd asked the previous day. 'Last vicar beat the devil round the gooseberry bush he did, with his shaggy-dog stories.'

Will had promised her he tried to restrict his sermons to five minutes, but Mrs Pipe had clucked her tongue sceptically and muttered something about that being 'dubersome'.

Now it was evening, and Will and Serena were in the study while Ashna, despite encouragement to join the pair of them, was in her room reading the first of a stack of English classics Serena had lent her. Serena was also reading a novel, stretched out on the sofa beside the newly installed log burner, which was exuding a slightly smoky aroma and crackled comfortingly. As their first and immediate act of renovation they'd decided to install one of these stoves in the front hall as well as in the study and, aside from the kitchen (which had the warmth of the Rayburn), they now didn't venture into any other downstairs room. They got through an enormous amount of logs, but as long as the burners were kept going, the difference to the temperature was astonishing. With the place feeling cosier, Serena decided it was a home made for winter. She could just imagine it all dressed up to the nines at Christmas time – under normal circumstances anyway. She wasn't sure if she'd ever want to celebrate that time of year again as things stood.

She took off her reading glasses and put her book down beside her. 'Will,' she said.

'Mmm,' he replied, not looking up.

'Do you mind having Ashna here?'

Will put his papers to one side, giving up on his preparation for now. 'Of course not,' he replied. 'She's a breath of fresh air, and a comfort for you, I think?'

Serena nodded, twisting her blonde curls around her finger as she often did. 'Well, it's got me thinking,' she went on. 'The house is still so vast even with the three of us now. And we could do with some extra money – the renovation's going to cost a fortune, even if we do try to cut corners. I wonder whether we should advertise for another lodger. A paying one. What do you think?'

Will took a sip of his gin and tonic and thought for a moment, his fiery head of hair tipped to one side. 'I think it's a brilliant idea,' he said at last, gently jumping on her suggestion. 'But we'll need to vet them carefully. We've all got to be able to live together. Ashna too must have a say. Do you think you could organise an advert in the local paper?' He didn't want to push Serena, but it seemed that she might, at last, be turning a corner, her energy returning a little.

'I'll do it on Monday,' she smiled, returning to her book. Will breathed an inward sigh of relief. There was a sparkle to that smile he hadn't seen in months. Slowly, he hoped, they were getting there.

Unfortunately, the response to the advert was not overwhelming – only one person applied and he was fresh out of prison. Will and Serena were unsure whether even to invite him for an interview, but Ashna gently commented that everyone deserved a second chance and, suitably chastened, they arranged for Pete Milton to meet the three of them the following evening.

Will, Serena and Ashna sat nervously by the fire in the study as they waited for Pete to arrive. Serena expected him to be late, but on the dot of seven the doorbell rang.

'I'll go,' said Will.

Serena and Ashna sat in silence as they tried to hear what was being said in the hallway. There was laughter, which was heartening. They smiled at each other. The next moment, Will and the stranger made their way into the study, Will carrying a bottle of wine.

'Look,' Will said to Serena. 'This is Pete and he's very kindly brought us a bottle of red.'

'No idea about wine, I'm afraid, so it could be rubbish, but the bloke at the grocer's down the road asked me who it was for and when I told him, he said: "*The new vicar is partial to a full-bodied red. I suggest the Claret. This one was an* exceptionally *good year.*"'

Serena giggled. Pete's impression of the rather particular and well-spoken grocer was spot on, even though Pete's own accent was true Essex.

Serena introduced Pete to Ashna, explaining that she was a lodger as well.

'Where are you from?' asked Ashna as Will ran downstairs to find some glasses and a corkscrew. Serena threw another log on the fire.

'Essex. Chelmsford. I'm a proper Essex boy.'

'No way! That's where I'm from too. Guess that makes me an Essex girl,' Ashna said, smiling shyly.

Serena observed the pair of them with interest. She couldn't help but feel the flicker of her famous matchmaking tendencies rising to the surface. She'd always enjoyed pairing people up, with some success: she'd managed to fix up her friend Lisa with a lovely Aussie she'd gone on to marry.

And both Ashna and Pete were stunning. Pete had dark blue eyes that shone like sapphires, just like Will's, although his colouring was otherwise very different. He was as dark as Will was fair, with an enviable olive skin tone, and where Will had a thick thatch of red hair, Pete's was dark and cropped very short. Serena thought he must be close in age to Ashna. Mid-twenties at the most. A decade younger than her and Will.

The evening turned out to be a scream. They opened the red and drank at least two more bottles between the four of them. Ashna had never drunk alcohol before living at the Vicarage, but had soon become accustomed to the joys of a glass of wine.

By eleven that night, they'd all agreed Pete could move in. It was true he'd recently served time for his participation in an armed robbery, but he promised he'd very much seen the error of his ways and instinctively they all knew that was the case.

Serena had been a bit worried about asking him why he'd been in prison – she didn't want to embarrass him – but Pete had been very open and honest.

'I know it doesn't make it any better really, but I was the get-away driver. My cousin and his mates decided to rob a bank and they roped me in. They'd never done nothin' like it before but they Googled what they needed to do. S'pose it's no surprise we were caught. Nobody got hurt, but my cousin's mate had a gun. Not that I knew that. They kept me in the dark about the details. I was just meant to drive them off. We got about half a mile down the road before the cops stopped us. My cousin and his mates got a longer stretch than me, but I still got four years. Served two, then managed to get parole. Not the best two years of my life, but the prison chaplain became a great mate. A solid bloke, he was. That's what made me get in touch when I saw your advert. Thought a vicar might see past the trouble I've been in. I only saw it by chance – my great-aunt lives nearby and I was round there mowin' the lawn for her when she showed me the ad. I've been stayin' with me parents but they don't want much to do with me any more. They're pretty well off these days – my dad's done well sellin' conservatories to all the commuters living in Essex. They've given me a bit of money to get me goin' with a fresh start, but they don't want me in sight,' he explained with a wry smile. 'I'll need to look for a job, but I've got enough to cover the rent for a few months. Seems like a nice village for a new beginning, anyway.'

'You'll be joining the club,' Serena told him, picking up her glass of wine. 'We're all new here. Me, Will, Ashna. A brand new start – together. Let's drink to that.' And they did.

※

The imminent arrival of an ex-con at the Vicarage caused a few raised eyebrows. Word had spread quickly in the small village and the day before Pete was due to move in, the staccato shrill of the doorbell startled Serena. She made her way up from the kitchen, only to jump again when it burst into life just as she was about to open the door.

'Sorry,' she apologised breathlessly. 'I still haven't got used to how huge the house is.' She smiled at the woman on her doorstep. 'Do come in,' she added, drawing back the door.

'Thank you. You must be the vicar's wife.'

'Actually, we're not married. Will calls me his lover,' Serena giggled.

'How very modern,' came the crisp reply. 'Allow me to introduce myself. Miss Dawson, churchwarden and, if I say so myself, a pillar of the church and local community.' She was ample, with thin silver hair, spectacles perched at the end of her nose, and below her chin was a turkey's wattle that wobbled disconcertingly when she spoke.

'I saw the vicar at the church yesterday. I was arranging the flowers for Sunday. He didn't mention you would be taking in a lodger,' she added, disapprovingly. Serena was slightly taken aback. She hadn't realised quite how much input country parishioners would expect to have in their lives.

'Please, come and have a cup of tea,' she said, ignoring the accusation. 'This way,' she added, although she imagined Miss Dawson probably knew the Vicarage better than Serena herself, being such a stalwart of the parish.

Busying herself around the kitchen, trying to remember where she'd put the sugar and locating a jug for the milk, Serena did her best to make small talk with Miss Dawson until finally the tea was made and she was forced to take a seat opposite the formidable woman.

'I'd already heard you'd taken on a *foreign* girl to help in the house,' remarked Miss Dawson once Serena had sat down. 'But I was even more alarmed to discover you interviewed an ex-convict as a potential lodger! I do hope you gave him short shrift,' she said, blowing on her tea delicately. The wattle wobbled.

'Actually, he's charming,' replied Serena. 'He moves in tomorrow. Poor lad, he got in with a terrible crowd in his youth, but he's a reformed character now. He's a good Christian and I'm sure you'll be as bowled over by him as we all are,' she said, more confidently than she felt.

'A leopard never changes its spots,' Miss Dawson predicted. 'He'll be off with the silver before you know it.'

'Oh, Miss Dawson, we don't even have any silver,' Serena said, laughing. 'And you'll be as familiar as I am with the concepts of forgiveness and redemption,' she added, feeling ashamed to think that it had taken Ashna to remind her of this. The comment was perhaps a tiny bit barbed as well, as Serena was starting to become a little fed up with Miss Dawson by now.

'Well, don't say I didn't warn you,' came the reply, and this time Serena bit her tongue.

'Now, Miss Dawson,' she said, changing tack. 'You're so familiar with the goings-on in the village, I'm sure you'll be a great help to us as we settle in. Perhaps you could tell me what events take place through the year so I can be sure we follow tradition as much as possible. Let me get a notepad.'

Miss Dawson brightened considerably at this, perhaps relieved to discover the young new vicar and his girlfriend wouldn't be too radical after all, even if they were living in sin, taking in an 'Injun' girl (as pronounced by Miss Dawson) and harbouring an (ex-) convict. She settled back in her chair and began to rattle off the parish's annual events as Serena scribbled away in the notepad. Miss Dawson was particularly enthusiastic about the Harvest Supper, which took place annually in October, and Serena's heart sank as she realised it would be up to her and Will to match up to what had clearly always been a very popular event. It sounded like a very posh affair – a cocktail party with waitresses offering round canapés while a string quartet provided the music.

An hour later Serena saw Miss Dawson off the premises. She returned to the kitchen, washed the teacups (she wasn't sure she'd ever get used to not having a dishwasher) and then she ripped her list from the notepad and tore it neatly into shreds.

6.
SUMMER 1990

Serena was as pleased as the next child at the prospect of the summer holidays, but there was one aspect of them she wasn't so thrilled about. She and Freddie, her pen pal, had been exchanging letters on a weekly basis now since April and he'd warned her in his last letter that, with his return to Majorca for the summer holidays, it was unlikely he'd have much time to write until term began again in September. Writing to Freddie and, even better, receiving his letters had become a source of enormous joy for Serena.

There had, of course, been a battle with Luna about it at first, as her sister had wanted to write to him as well. Serena had caved in as usual and Luna had written a long letter that was much more amusing than Serena's. But Luna had lost interest even before buying a stamp and soon it became clear to Serena that her twin would never have the patience to establish a long-distance friendship. She was far too much of an immediate, impulsive person.

It was strange how different Luna was from the rest of the family. Both girls looked like their mother Stephanie, who was tall and slim with blonde hair she tamed as best she could. And, like Stephanie, Luna was interested in clothes and a good gossip, but otherwise Luna and her mother were dissimilar. Luna was passionate and moody, while Stephanie was a far milder and more even-tempered person, although Serena supposed that came at a price: she could be somewhat detached and unemotional, very involved in her own life and in keeping up appearances.

Their father, meanwhile, was a considered, cautious character. He loved butterflies and pored over his lepidopterology books, teaching Serena which winged creatures to look out for on their walks together. She'd recognised a rare Green Hairstreak on their last ramble, much to Arthur's delight.

He was also obsessed with making tiny model aircraft, working tirelessly at the desk in his study as he painstakingly glued and painted each model. Serena often brought her beanbag through to the study to watch him deftly working at his passion. It wasn't the subject that magnetised Serena, but the delicate way in which her father's nimble fingers worked and the intensity of his eyes. She found herself immersed in a kind of trance as she sat quietly, observing. It was her favourite thing to do.

Luna thought them both strange – Serena and their father. She endlessly tried to make her twin more like her. To encourage her out of the study and up to the bedroom they shared, trying to entice her with glittery nail varnishes or an offer for Serena to cut her doll's hair. But Serena remained where she was until Luna gave up and soon she would burst into the study, her face caked in a mud pack, hoping to scare Arthur and Serena with her ghoulish looks. They would both smile obligingly, but their attention would soon return to the model aircraft and Luna would give up, wash off her mask and retreat to the kitchen to discuss outfits with their mum.

In truth, Serena thought six weeks was a little long and by the end of August she was yearning to return to school and the structure it offered. Too much of life at home was unpredictable. Her father was an anchor of solidity, but on weekdays he left early to catch his train for work in the City and didn't return until gone six, when he'd retreat to his study with a stiff drink and only emerge at suppertime. Stephanie, meanwhile, was always rushing off to luncheon parties or tennis games or her book club, leaving Mrs Horrins from next door installed in the sitting room with her tapestry to keep an eye on the girls.

Serena was thus left to fend for herself in the strange world of Luna's moods. Serena was fairly sure she was exactly the same person every day. Not very exciting, perhaps, but somebody perfectly obedient and capable of pleasant conversation with anyone she might come across. With Luna, however, you could never be sure who she might be from one day to the next. There could be a day so blissful Serena hardly dared breathe in case she broke the spell: a day when Luna and she would play cheerfully with their Barbie dolls in their bedroom or splash around in the paddling pool in the garden. But the next one, for no apparent reason, would be the polar opposite and Serena would observe scowls from across the breakfast table and find herself losing her appetite, her toast lodging itself in her chest in a hard lump, aware that the day ahead would be long and testing.

The worst were the days when her sister announced she was 'having a bad day,' as she would describe it, making Serena feel somehow at fault. Anything could prompt this. Occasionally it was justified, but more often than not Luna's behaviour was out of proportion. Once, Louise Bradbury invited Serena to her birthday party and not Luna, causing an almighty storm in the Meadows household. Serena had to endure her sister's sulks, glares and much slamming of doors all day long until in the end, in despair, she phoned Louise and asked if she'd mind inviting Luna too.

'But I did invite her!' Louise said. 'I sent you an invitation each. I thought it must be annoying always getting joint ones. Hers must have got lost in the post.'

Serena relayed this to Luna who was initially suspicious, but after speaking to Louise herself, relented at last. Louise sent her another invitation and Serena felt as though she could breathe again, but she could barely believe it when Luna then declined to attend.

'I'm afraid I'm busy that day,' she wrote on her RSVP slip. She was the queen of cutting off her nose to spite her face.

Serena wished sometimes she had the guts to ruin one of the good days by insisting she was 'having a bad day' herself, but she never dared, and never really even wanted to.

So when the holidays came to an end, it was with relief that Serena returned to school, even though she wouldn't be in Miss Jones's class any longer. And her first day back was made even more wonderful by the arrival of a letter with a Spanish postage stamp, waiting for her as she scrambled through the front door at the end of the day.

'*Dear Serena,*' the letter began. '*I'm not even back at school yet but I thought I'd write anyway. The holidays haven't been as much fun as I expected this year – two of my sisters are staying with friends and I've been a bit bored with just Little Jane for company. In a strange way, I'll be looking forward to getting back to the dorm! Anyway, you're probably mega busy but I thought I'd take five minutes to scribble a quick letter to you . . .*'

Serena hugged the letter to her chest. Back to normality. To routine. To letters from Freddie.

7.
MARCH 2015

Three weeks after moving into the Vicarage the new household had settled into a routine together. Will was an early bird and was always up and about hours before anyone else, walking to the shop to buy a newspaper, and chatting with other early risers in the parish, but Serena and Ashna had taken to breakfasting together and Pete would often join them as they were finishing up.

After that, Pete would head off to the bus stop and journey into Rye for a demoralising morning at the job centre while Serena and Ashna companionably completed various chores around the house, occasionally assisted by Mrs Pipe. Serena had yet to work the mysterious housekeeper out. There was something dreadfully creepy about her and yet she could be amusing too, in a deadpan sort of way. Ashna seemed a little nervous of her and would sometimes make excuses when Mrs Pipe was there, disappearing to her room. She seemed to spend a lot of time in there but Serena was reluctant to disturb her, although every now and then she would try to encourage her to talk.

One day, when Ashna was about to vanish again, Serena asked if she'd mind helping her sort out the laundry room. All the bedding was still in boxes and needed unpacking and stacking in neat piles. Ashna was more than happy to help, but was content to do so without much chatter.

'How are you settling in?' Serena asked her as they folded sheets and blankets. 'Do you like the village?'

'It's lovely, from what I've seen so far. I get a bit panicky when I go out and about. At the moment I'd rather stay in the house. It's so kind of you to let me stay.'

'Not at all. I'm sorry you don't feel able to get out more though. Your family won't know you're here, Ashna. You're not going to bump into them in the village.'

'The sensible part of me knows that, but I'm just so scared . . . Am I going to spend the rest of my life looking over my shoulder? I can't bear it.' Ashna's eyes were wide and afraid.

'Ashna, I understand . . . But you've got to live. You're only young.' Serena stopped herself. She was preaching to someone who was injured and needed time to lick her wounds. If anyone understood that, she did.

'Will you help me with this sheet?' she asked, changing the conversation, and Ashna smiled with relief.

'Of course.'

And although Serena worried about her, Ashna seemed happy enough when she joined the rest of them for dinner each night, which was generally an extremely jolly affair, with Will providing the evening meal and Pete always full of light-hearted chatter despite his lack of success on the job front.

The beginnings of spring were becoming apparent at last and, on a particularly mild day in March, Serena turned thirty-five. She hadn't made any plans this year. The only thing she wished of the day was that it should come and go like any other.

It soon became clear her birthday wish would not be granted. She'd barely woken when she was greeted by a wide-grinned Will, carrying a cup of tea in one hand and with a large grey cat under the other arm.

'Happy birthday to you!' he sang out, depositing the tea on the pine bedside table and the cat on the bed.

'Oh, it's adorable!' Serena exclaimed, inspecting the grey ball of fluff. 'Has it got a name?'

'Not it, she,' replied Will as he perched on the bed. 'And she's called Paddington. Makes her sound like a boy, but she was deposited at the rescue centre with a sign round her neck saying "*Please look after this cat*", hence the name. She looks quite like a bear, I think.'

'Oh, she does! And she's so cuddly, look!' Serena had by now gathered the cat to her, cradling her like a baby.

'The most sweet-natured cat they had,' Will explained. 'And I admit, there's another reason for Paddington. I didn't want to freak you out, but the other day I saw a mouse in the kitchen. I thought Paddington could earn her keep.'

'I *thought* I heard a squeaking noise in the kitchen yesterday. Well, Paddington, you're a truly wonderful present. Thank you so much,' she said, looking at Will and marvelling for the millionth time at how lucky she was to have him. He looked pleased as punch to have thought of such a clever idea and she loved how transparent he was. He'd been open and straightforward from the moment she'd first met him.

'Now,' said Will, as he took a slurp of Serena's tea. 'Have you thought about how you're going to spend your morning?'

'No plans,' she answered. 'Unpack a few more boxes. Nearly done now. And I thought I'd ring round to see if I can get a quote from a painter and decorator.'

'Excellent, but don't forget to have some fun too,' Will told her as he slipped on his dog collar. 'I'm busy this morning but I'll pop back for a bite to eat at lunchtime. Don't go to any trouble though, there's plenty in the fridge.'

❧

Will got back, as promised, at one o'clock just as Serena was rustling about in the fridge looking for the salad dressing.

'No need for that,' Will said, wrapping his arm around Serena's waist and pushing the fridge door shut. 'I'm taking you out, come on.'

'Really?' asked Serena. Despite her advice to Ashna, she hadn't ventured out much herself since they'd moved to the village. She was taking things slowly – still fragile, though she was gradually beginning to feel better in this new environment. So far she'd had outings only to the church on Sundays, the grocer's and the newsagent's.

'Where are we going?' Serena asked as she applied her lip gloss in the hallway mirror. It was her only nod to make-up – she'd never quite managed to get the hang of it, despite numerous lessons from her sister. Will draped her parka over her shoulders.

'You'll see,' he answered, and five minutes later they were entering the local pub where a table had been beautifully decorated with balloons and banners. On one of the placemats was a pile of presents. Serena was touched, but confused too, for the table was laid for seven – not two.

'Surprise!' shouted Ashna as she emerged from under the table. Serena looked on in amusement as Pete then also appeared, ludicrously, from underneath while Mrs Pipe stepped out silently from behind a curtain, making Serena jump. A couple she'd never met before hovered slightly awkwardly, having clearly decided to maintain their dignity and refrain from hiding with the others.

'Serena, this is Dr Charles,' Ashna explained. 'You remember? He was the kind stranger who gave me a lift to the Vicarage.'

34

'Of course,' said Serena, shaking his hand. He was middle-aged – approaching fifty, she'd have guessed – but had a definite gleam in his eye that made him seem younger.

'Please, call me Rob. And this is my wife, Alice,' the doctor explained. Serena took the cool, limp hand of a woman who must have been in her early forties and who clearly took great care of herself. She was dressed impeccably, with toned arms that suggested hours on the tennis court or in the gym, carefully highlighted coppery hair (as sleek as Serena's was messy), perfect make-up and pale blue eyes.

'It's so sweet of you to come,' said Serena. 'Especially as you haven't even met us before!' Alice gave a tight smile, but Rob waved his arms around as though it were nothing.

'Always love a party,' he said. 'And a party is never a party without this,' he declared, as he grabbed a bottle from the stainless steel bucket on the table and popped open the champagne.

'Happy birthday!' he brayed, and the celebration really began.

'It was so kind of you to give Ashna a lift to the Vicarage,' Serena said to Rob as they clinked glasses, both of them observing Ashna, who was chatting to Pete by the bar.

'Not at all! I felt guilty that I didn't invite her to stay with us, but Alice was away that evening and you know how villagers can talk.' He cleared his throat. 'I thought it better all round if she tried the Vicarage first, though I did give her my number just in case.'

'She said. You did the right thing, anyway. We're thrilled to have her.'

Alice had been talking to Will, but at this point she joined Serena and Rob, cradling a glass of mineral water.

'What's the story with . . . I'm sorry – what's her name?' Alice asked.

'Ashna,' Serena told her. 'I'll let her tell you herself, but she was in need of a place to stay and Will and I were delighted to start filling some of the rooms in the Vicarage. We have Pete now too. I'll introduce you in a minute.'

'Well, don't fill every room with lodgers,' laughed Rob. 'You two young things . . . I expect there'll be the pitter-patter of tiny feet soon.'

Serena noticed Alice shoot the doctor a warning glance and she warmed to her a little more. Fortunately, before Serena had a chance to answer, Will appeared at her elbow.

'Come on then, birthday girl, take a seat. Time to order some food.'

❧

By four o'clock, Serena had opened all her gifts and everyone was marvellously sozzled in spite of their fine lunches – apart from Alice who needed to drive to the local prep school to pick up her children, Toby and Emily. She left them all to it, a look of relief on her face, while Serena refilled her glass. She couldn't remember the last time she'd drunk this much in the daytime and it felt liberating – she felt like a champagne bottle after it's been uncorked. She noticed Will also looked more relaxed than he had in months. He was chatting enthusiastically to Pete, who was concentrating hard as Will explained how he'd started home-brewing beer, going into all the scientific details.

'How long does it take to make?' asked Pete.

'The initial fermenting process takes up to a couple of weeks.'

'But how do you know if it's ready to bottle?'

'There's two ways to tell – if bubbles come out of the airlock at a rate of less than one every ten minutes, it's more than likely ready. And if the yeast's settling at the bottom, leaving the beer clear rather than hazy – that's another indicator it's all set.'

Serena switched off at this point, but Pete looked completely in awe. Turning away from this riveting discussion, Serena observed her other companions around the table, feeling a warm glow, until she began to overhear Mrs Pipe's conversation with Ashna who was looking distinctly uncomfortable.

'A-cursed, so they say,' Mrs Pipe said, a dark look on her face.

'What's that?' asked Serena, scraping her chair closer to the housekeeper.

'Oh, I don't know I should say,' she said, clamming up.

'Come on,' said Serena, smiling. 'You were telling Ashna. Why not me?'

Mrs Pipe cleared her throat. 'Well, it may be nonsense, but the story goes there's a curse on the Vicarage. There was a vicar with a roving eye, 'ad affairs all round the village, he did. Then his long-suffering wife died in childbirth in the house. Legend has it, the place has been a-cursed ever since. A baby's not lived in that house since she died over a hundred years ago.'

'That can't be true,' Serena said, smiling too brightly. She could see Will from the corner of her eye. He had clearly overheard and looked like he might throttle Mrs Pipe. 'After all,' Serena continued, 'the last vicar and his wife had four children.'

'Oh, aye,' agreed Mrs Pipe, 'but the youngest were five when they moved in. The vicar's wife before her was a fresh young thing. Never did bear a child herself. They ended up adopting a teenager,' she said, nodding sagely.

Serena began to feel too hot, her cheeks burning. She needed to get out of the pub, to get home.

'Are you okay?' asked Ashna, her dark eyes concerned.

'Fine, I'm fine,' said Serena. 'I've had too much to drink, that's all. I'm not used to drinking at lunchtime. I might just get some air,' she said, gathering her coat and bag.

She raced out of the pub, running all the way home where she scooped up Paddington and retreated to the bedroom. Will found her twenty minutes later, a look of contrition on his face.

'I'm so sorry,' he said, rubbing his forehead. Will looked tired – exhausted – and Serena was furious with herself for putting him through this. She had to move on. She simply had to.

'It was a lovely lunch,' Serena told him sincerely. 'I just got a bit overwhelmed by Mrs Pipe's story.'

'You don't believe it, do you?' asked Will. He was so pragmatic. He was spiritual, of course, but he had no truck with superstition.

'Of course not,' replied Serena. 'It's just . . . you know, with everything that's happened . . .'

'You've got to just dismiss this, Serena. We have to move on. I so desperately want us to get back to how we were. Please promise me you won't think any more about it?' Will pleaded.

'I promise,' Serena told him. But later, when Will was downstairs, she made her way along to the old nursery. She breathed in deeply. The room smelt musty, unlived in. When had this nursery last been home to a baby? Something about the room made her not just sad, but uneasy. There was a stillness to it. What was it Mrs Pipe had said?

'Legend has it, the place has been a-cursed ever since. A baby's not lived in that house since she died over a hundred years ago . . .'

'No!' Serena shouted into the dense and fusty atmosphere. 'Please, no!'

She turned from the room, slammed the door and stumbled along to her bedroom, tears rolling down her cheeks.

When will our luck change? Serena despaired inwardly. She could barely believe that the very place supposed to heal them both, to give them their new beginning, now appeared to be cursed – and in a way that couldn't have been more significant to Serena. *'A baby's not lived in that house since she died over a hundred years ago . . .'*

It couldn't have been much worse.

8.
SUMMER 1996

Two days after they finished their GCSEs, Luna announced she'd been invited to stay with Claudia Wrentham in Singapore for the month of August. Claudia was the most glamorous girl at their school and her father, a merchant banker, had recently been headhunted for a job at a multinational company in the Far East. He and Claudia's mother had moved to Singapore in May, with their daughter to follow on after finishing her exams. Claudia had stayed with the Meadows while she took her exams.

'Am I invited?' asked Serena, although she knew she wouldn't be and wasn't too disappointed. Luna pulled a face.

'Sorry, Serena,' she said. 'Just me.' Luna didn't look sorry at all.

'The airfare will be expensive,' said their father, looking over his newspaper. 'Are you expecting your mother and me to stump up for it?' he asked sternly.

'Well, I did wonder if you might,' wheedled Luna. 'After all, you paid for Serena to have all that extra tuition in maths that I didn't need,' she added triumphantly.

'Hardly the same,' muttered Arthur, but he looked defeated already. Serena wished that sometimes, just sometimes, her parents would stand up to Luna properly.

As August approached, Serena found herself encountering mixed feelings about Luna's imminent departure. It would be the first time in their lives they'd been apart and, although half of her was relieved at the prospect, she still felt knitted to Luna in a way that made her panic more and more as the trip approached. She also hated the thought of being left behind, with nothing remotely exciting to do. And then a thought struck her.

It was a humid July day and Serena dashed upstairs to her bedroom to sit at her computer, even though the room was far too stuffy in such weather. She switched on the terminal and waited patiently for it to boot up. Eventually she was able to log into her email account.

'*Hi, Freddie,*' she began to write. '*Don't suppose you fancy a visitor this summer, do you?*' she followed on, boldly.

Serena and Freddie were still pen pals, even after all this time. They didn't write weekly any more and their missives were no longer sent by snail mail, but they emailed each other every month or so. They'd each found that having never met in person meant they opened up to one another in a way they wouldn't with their other friends. It was cathartic – like strangers on a train.

They had actually tried to meet up on a couple of occasions over the last year, but somehow it had never quite worked out – the first time Serena had been struck down with a sickness bug and then Freddie had broken his ankle in a hockey match the day they'd planned to have lunch. Perhaps it would be a case of third time lucky.

Serena sat at the desk, waiting for a response, refreshing the computer screen every five minutes until her bottom went numb. In the end, she went downstairs and helped herself to a cold Coke. When she returned to her bedroom, there was an email in her inbox.

'*You bet! August would be a good time, if that suits you? Mum says you're more than welcome and all my sisters will be here so you'll see them too. I can't believe that we're actually going to get to meet, as long as neither of us gets sick!'*

She logged off, marched determinedly downstairs and, without much persuasion at all, her mother agreed. Serena was going to Majorca.

9.
MARCH 2015

Late on her birthday, after she'd calmed down, Serena went to find Will, feeling they needed to discuss the significance of the reputed curse further. She went downstairs, but he wasn't there so she searched the whole house, eventually finding him in one of the attic rooms. She was about to go in when she realised he had a white box in his arms.

'There it is,' Will said to himself as he placed the box carefully on the ground and started to look through its contents. A toy elephant – unisex, he'd said to Serena when he'd brought it home from the shop the day after the twelve-week scan. For the same reason, he'd bought yellow and green babygros with little ducks on them, and a tiny pair of knitted bootees he hadn't been able to resist. Underneath all of this, the scan photos. Serena saw Will take one out of the envelope and look at it for several minutes. After a while the picture began to shake in his hand. Tears ran down his face, but his sobs were silent.

'Enough!' Will reprimanded himself at last. He blew his nose with a hanky, then piled the items back into the box and hid it high up in a cupboard. Serena's heart ached for him. For all that he'd told her it was time to move on, it was clear he wasn't even close to getting there himself. She turned and crept away.

A week later Serena decided to put all thoughts of curses out of her mind – although she was avoiding the nursery like the plague. In need of distraction, she decided it was finally time to set about revamping the Vicarage now that they'd fully unpacked.

Ashna kept very much to herself, not wishing to intrude on Will and Serena, but on a sunny March day Serena decided she was in need of Ashna's help with making a list of what needed to be done in the house. She knocked gently on Ashna's bedroom door.

'Come in,' came Ashna's soft tones.

'I'm sorry to disturb you,' apologised Serena as she opened the door. She paused, taken aback, for the room was strewn with the most exquisitely vibrant scarves and bedspreads.

'Ashna!' she exclaimed, absorbing the kaleidoscope of colours around her. 'These are beautiful!'

Ashna looked embarrassed. 'Thanks,' she said. 'It's what I've been up to since I got here. It keeps me busy. Mrs Pipe finds me old material from jumble sales and so on and I use that as my base for these,' she explained.

'But they're amazing,' said Serena, touching a turquoise scarf embellished with rich gold embroidery. 'Do you sell them? You could make a fortune. I can't believe they're made from recycled rags!'

'I've just started to sell a few through the antiques and interiors shop, to get a little income. I want to start contributing some rent. The guy who owns it says they make good gifts. I have something here for you, actually – I'm afraid it wasn't quite ready on your birthday.'

Ashna rummaged around in the drawer beside her bed and handed Serena a wrapped parcel. Serena quickly unpeeled the paper, revealing a sea-green scarf with silver thread sewn through it.

'Oh, I love it!' gasped Serena, draping the scarf round her neck immediately and checking her reflection in Ashna's mirror. 'It matches my eyes exactly. Ashna, you're so talented! How did you learn to do this – are you trained?'

'Yes . . . I went to a technical college after school and studied textiles.'

'Your parents let you?'

'Yes, though it was pretty restricted. I was escorted to college and back by my brother and I wasn't allowed to mix with anyone on my course or socialise with them. But at least I was doing something I'm passionate about. My mother fought for me to be able to take the course. I was so grateful to her.'

'You miss her,' Serena said gently.

Ashna nodded, but she'd said enough. Serena understood.

'Now, I'm guessing you needed me?' Ashna asked, changing the subject.

'Oh, yes, I'd totally forgotten. Ashna, I think it's time to set about improving the Vicarage. I need to go round the house making a list. Will you help me?'

'Of course,' said Ashna, putting down her needle and thread. 'I've been desperate to get started, but I didn't want to push you. Come on, let's begin at the top.'

Serena hesitated for a moment, reticent to return to the scene of Will's distress, but then she realised she was being silly. She was avoiding the nursery as it was. She didn't want the entire house to end up out of bounds. The two women climbed up to the top floor and looked around. Ashna's eyes were eager and Serena soon caught her enthusiasm for the project, however overwhelming it seemed.

'Now, the first thing we need to bear in mind is that the property's bound to be listed,' said Ashna as she inspected the attic windows.

'Of course! I hadn't even thought of that,' replied Serena, her heart sinking. How did this young girl know so much?

'I love all those shows on TV, if you're wondering,' Ashna explained. 'Don't tell anyone,' she stage-whispered, 'but I've got a real thing for Phil Spencer from *Location, Location, Location*!'

Serena giggled. 'I love that programme too,' she agreed and they decided to settle down to watch it together on Thursday.

But for now the Vicarage required their attention. In the end, although the wind whistled in through the rattling sash windows, Serena and Ashna decided they were basically sound and that to try to restore them would be far too costly. A lick of paint was all this floor really needed. They also needed to think of some use for the attic rooms, which were currently bare of any furnishings.

'How about a sewing room for you for starters?' suggested Serena.

'Oh, I couldn't! This is your house. I can't take over,' replied Ashna, but Serena was insistent.

'Far better than crowding out your bedroom with all that beautiful material. And anyway, it's not safe. What if you stood on a pin in the night?' Serena added and so it was agreed that the largest of the attic rooms would become a small workspace for Ashna, with the other rooms used for storage, although Serena thought she might install a couple of second-hand beds just in case they ever had a houseful.

Back down on the first floor, more work was required. Ashna noted that each room needed the ancient floral wallpaper to be stripped and replaced with a decent coat of paint and that the parquet floor on the landing needed a good polish. The carpets in the bedrooms were decent enough, although Ashna noticed there was a large stain on the one in the nursery.

'Let's just leave that for now,' said Serena, closing the door firmly, and Ashna didn't argue.

In the master bedroom, the original fireplace remained and Serena was contemplating getting this unblocked, as the room was icy at this time of year and she'd always thought it would be incredibly romantic to have a flickering fire casting a warm and cosy glow on their bed. Otherwise, it was in reasonable condition and the modern en suite was plain and clean. The dressing room could do with more shelving though, and Ashna listed this on her notepad.

Pete was in his room and they decided not to disturb him, so they headed downstairs again. Serena found she was by now quite into her stride.

'The staircase will need a good polish too. And down here, some of these need replacing,' she added, pointing out a couple of cracked flagstones in the entrance hall. There was more painting required both on the ground and basement floors.

When the two of them entered the kitchen, Serena slumped down onto a chair.

'What on earth do we do in here?' she asked, casting her eye over the room, which was in dire need of a lick of paint and so old-fashioned as to be almost prehistoric. The huge central work table was the main feature of the room, but it was heavily stained and rife with indentations from slicing and chopping.

'You're not going to put in modern kitchen units, are you?' asked Ashna. 'It's so charming as it is.' Serena looked over the kitchen again, as if with fresh eyes.

'I think I'd rather not, especially as the floor would be ruined – the tessellated tiles are too beautiful to rip up. Such incredible blues and golds. I suppose if we had the central work table cleaned up professionally that would be a start,' she conceded.

'And the dresser is rather lovely,' she observed, getting up to inspect it. It was made of pine and there were cup hooks along the edges of the shelves, as well as narrow grooves along the tops, where pretty plates could be stored while on display. 'Historical, even,' Serena added, making a mental note to seek out some attractive crockery when she was next at a second-hand shop.

'Exactly!' enthused Ashna, and soon they agreed simply to make small changes to the room, retaining its old-fashioned charm as much as possible.

By the end of the day, Serena had contacted a local painter and decorator – she never had got round to it on her birthday – and arranged to meet him the day after next. By the time she climbed into bed, wrapping her arms around Will's solid torso, she was exhausted. The next day she woke feeling fresh. It was the best night's sleep she'd had in many, many months.

10.
AUGUST 1996

For the first two days of her holiday in Majorca, Serena felt miserably homesick. She was mystified as to why, since she'd been so looking forward to the trip. She could understand feeling homesick for her father, but it wasn't just him she missed. She missed her uncosy mother, her bedroom, the faulty tap that dripped in the next-door bathroom all night – even Luna's changeable moods. It made no sense and yet Arthur had always instilled in his girls that blood was thicker than water. It was one of the few matters he was adamant about, having been fostered throughout his childhood until finding his twin brother in his teens and discovering they were almost identical, not just in looks but in character. Serena now realised that perhaps her father was right. Despite everything, she missed her family more than she'd ever thought possible.

She was a polite girl, however, and tried her best to conceal her longing for home from her hosts, who ran a bed and breakfast business from the farmhouse, or *finca* as they called it.

Freddie's Mum, Bobbi, seemed to sense that this girl with wild blonde locks was rather lost and put the kinder of Freddie's older sisters in charge of bolstering her spirits. And soon enough, Serena found herself enjoying being part of a large and energetic family.

Bobbi was a very tranquil kind of person. She had long, youthful dark hair and a worn but attractive face, tanned to walnut by the sun. She wore long skirts and beads and everything she did was done at a slow, measured pace. She reminded Serena of her father and she found herself watching, mesmerised, as Bobbi went about her daily tasks. She was enchanting, whatever she was doing – collecting the hens' eggs, laying the long wooden table on the terrace, hanging sheets on the washing line, brushing her hair with steady even strokes, screwing in her chunky earrings. Always busy. Never idle. But her industry took place in such an unrushed and soothing manner.

Freddie's father too was laid-back, but he had a different energy about him. He also looked like an old hippy, with long faded hair, a beard and droopy clothes – but Freddie had explained to Serena in one of his letters that Malcolm used to be a City trader, and there was a sparky liveliness about him that made it possible to imagine him shouting out numbers in the pit, pacing around with a phone clamped to his ear. But the City was always a means to an end for him and as soon as he had enough money he left London, family in tow, to live out his lifelong dream of subsisting somewhere warm and undemanding.

Freddie's older sisters were called Amber and Ebony, such exotic names that Serena couldn't understand why his little sister was called Jane. In fact, she was always known as 'Little Jane' as she was a tiny little thing, looking much younger than her eleven years. Freddie himself was a little older than Serena at seventeen and the two older girls were close in age – Ebony nineteen and Amber twenty. Neither of them seemed to have a job or to be in any sort of education. They just sauntered around the house, sporadically helping their parents out with the bed and breakfast business in the day and partying hard at night.

As for Freddie himself, it had been a revelation to Serena to discover the character traits not yet revealed through his letters, most notably his fearlessness. He was wild. Perhaps even reckless. And yet courteous as well, conscious not to let this part of his character impact on anyone else, including her. The very first time Serena saw him, arriving at the farmhouse after being picked up by Bobbi (who'd explained that Freddie was looking after his little sister, who got terribly carsick), he was flying through the air on his bike. He'd created some kind of homemade ramp in the garden and she watched as he pedalled at full speed towards it, took off into the air for several moments and landed with a gleeful holler. Though when he spotted Serena he quickly discarded his bike and ran over, eager to be introduced and show her around.

He was handsome too, incredibly so. She'd seen a photo, of course – he'd sent one with a letter recently – but clearly Freddie wasn't vain for the picture had done him no justice at all. Meanwhile, Serena feared the photo she'd sent of herself had been overly complimentary, catching her in a good light, and she wondered if Freddie thought her a disappointment in the flesh. Not that it mattered terribly. After all, it wasn't as though they were going out with each other. They were pen pals – nothing more, nothing less.

As the days passed, however, and Serena gradually felt more at home at the old *finca*, she had to admit she was growing increasingly attracted to Freddie. His olive skin grew darker by the day and his hair was a delicious combination of dark and light, with the effect of molten caramel. He was made for a hot country, she thought – unlike her. Her pale skin, unused to the sun, turned redder every day, no matter how much lotion she slapped on, and the heat made her hair frizz unattractively. One evening, Amber offered to lend Serena her hair straighteners and she attempted to iron out her springy curls along with the frizz. But while she thought she looked wonderfully grown-up and sophisticated, Freddie looked concerned when he saw her.

'Why are you trying to look like Amber and Ebs?' he asked, putting a hand out to touch her hair.

Serena felt her face begin to flame. 'I . . . I just thought I'd try a new style,' she stammered. 'Don't you like it?'

Freddie shrugged. 'It's nice, it's just . . .' he tailed off.

'What?' asked Serena, suddenly feeling a little cross. It had taken her ages to style her hair this way.

'You look like everyone else now,' he explained. 'I like you different.'

Then he grinned. 'But you do look good. Come on, let's go out tonight now you've made the effort. There's a bar you'll love. I'm sorry I haven't taken you out yet since you got here. Mum told me to give you time to settle in first. Majorca can be quite crazy when you're not used to it.'

Serena felt her spirits soar. By now she'd fallen in love with the old farmhouse in the hills of Deia, as well as with Freddie's family, but it would be exciting to sample the nightlife for which a part of the island was so famous. And going out with Freddie would be a kind of date, or so she hoped.

In fact, it was nothing like a date as it soon became clear Freddie had arranged to meet his older sisters and various friends at the bar, and the place was anything but intimate. The whole building vibrated with music and excitement and, although Serena was a little disappointed it wasn't just the two of them, she felt adrenaline start to flow through her body as she downed the beers she was handed on a regular basis by those who were old enough to buy them. By two o'clock in the morning, she was feeling very woozy indeed, but the bar had only just begun to fill. She stepped outside onto the cobbles to get some fresh air and, as she swayed outside the throbbing building, she savoured the warm breeze lifting her smoothed hair off her back.

'There you are!' It was Freddie. He'd found her. 'Don't go wandering off like that! I was worried,' he said. He didn't seem drunk at all, but Serena had seen him downing as many beers as she had. He watched her swaying and chuckled.

'Look at you,' he said, pulling her towards him, and Serena hoped he was about to kiss her. But he didn't. He just hugged her to him. It was a lovely hug – she felt safe and comforted – but sadly there was nothing romantic to it at all.

11.
MARCH 2015

Serena yawned. 'Right, time I went up. It's been fun though,' she added. She and Will had joined forces against Ashna and Pete for a game of *Pictionary*, which had been pretty raucous, fuelled by Will's homemade beer that he'd wanted everyone to sample. But it was late now and Serena's bed was calling.

'Me too,' agreed Ashna, hopping up off the floor where she'd been sitting on the rug beside the log burner, stroking Paddington, who'd been in seventh heaven.

'We'll just have a nightcap, shall we?' Will asked Pete as he jumped up and located a bottle of port. They were engrossed in conversation when the doorbell rang.

'It's late,' said Will, checking his watch. Almost midnight. 'Back in a sec,' he said to Pete.

Serena, having heard the doorbell, came downstairs, wrapped in a dressing gown. She watched as Will answered the door.

'Hello,' he said, greeting a scruffy-looking chap on the doorstep. The poor man looked cold and bedraggled, wearing just a thin anorak.

'You look freezing,' Will said. 'Come in and have a cup of tea,' he added, and the timid man followed him down the stairs, Serena trailing after them.

The man didn't say anything. He might well have been mute. But Will kept up a steady stream of undemanding chatter as he made him a cup of tea and heated up some soup while Serena found a couple of bread rolls and the butter dish. The man – clearly a vagrant – wolfed down the sustenance and stood up. He gave a little bow, then made his way back up the stairs, Will and Serena following behind.

'Wait!' said Will. 'Just hang on here a mo,' he added, and the poor soul stood and waited with Serena in the hall.

Will disappeared, returning with a thick Puffa jacket. 'I don't wear this any more,' he said. 'Would you like it?' The man looked at Will, gratitude in his eyes, and took the coat, quickly putting it on over his anorak.

Serena spotted Pete, who had emerged from the study and was watching this tender scene in wonder. Both Serena and Pete knew that Will wore that coat nearly every day. She had a feeling that Pete – who was in many ways still a child in comparison to Will and Serena – had decided then and there that when he grew up, he wanted to be just like Will.

The next morning, Serena and Ashna were at the kitchen table, waiting for the painter Serena had contacted to arrive, when Pete came down looking sleep-dishevelled.

'Mornin', ladies,' he said. They stared at him. How could anyone look so gorgeous when they'd just crawled out of bed? Pete flicked on the kettle, then scraped back a chair and plonked himself down, rubbing his eyes.

'What's this?' he asked, spotting Ashna's 'to do' list on the table.

'List of things that need doing to the house to get it looking remotely respectable,' said Serena, pulling a face. 'Only it's going to cost an arm and a leg. We're seeing a painter today, who I'm reliably informed is the cheapest in the business round here, but with the size of this place, I suspect the bill won't be for the faint-hearted.'

'You can have my arm and leg to pay for it, if you want,' Pete joked. 'I've always got another of each on the other side. I probably owe you a limb or two for takin' me in.'

Serena chuckled.

Will came in next and inspected the list himself. 'See if he can just do one floor at a time, to save us being too disrupted,' he said. 'Who'd like a coffee?' he asked then, noting the kettle had just boiled.

'Please, mate,' said Pete. He looked up at Will like a puppy to its master. Serena smiled. She could see why Pete was so in awe of Will, who, while kindly enough to have seen past his history, was no pushover. She felt as though she and Will were a little like an older brother and sister to Pete and Ashna. In fact, she couldn't believe how well the arrangement seemed to be working or how much better she felt for having more people in the house.

When the doorbell rang, Serena dashed up the stairs to answer it.

'Morning,' said the man at the door, who was wearing jeans and a checked shirt and had a remarkably well-spoken voice. He was tall, with a confident stance and a rugged complexion that suggested he spent a lot of time outdoors. His hair was thick and dark, cut short to tame the curls, and dark stubble – almost a beard – framed his smiling face.

'Hi,' said Serena, 'can I help you?' She wondered who this stranger might be. Knowing what vicarage life could be like, she couldn't begin to hazard whether this man would be looking for shelter, selling something or simply an old friend of Will's.

'We did say ten o'clock, didn't we?' the man asked, checking his watch.

'Oh, you're the painter!' Serena exclaimed. 'I'm sorry – it's just you don't look like one!'

'Overalls are in the van,' the man explained. 'It's the voice as well, isn't it? Bit posh for a painter and decorator,' he said, grinning cheerfully. 'Do you mind if I bring in the twins?' he asked next, and Serena shook her head. This was becoming more and more bizarre. He'd brought his children with him?

'I'll be down in the kitchen,' she shouted to the painter, who was by now approaching the back of the van parked opposite. He waved to assure her he'd heard.

'He's posh!' Serena informed the others as she scuttled down-stairs. Will laughed.

'Serena's a sucker for stereotyping,' he explained to Pete and Ashna. 'Always surprised if someone breaks the mould.'

'And he's bringing his children in with him,' she whispered now, in case the man was on his way down. The next moment, two lively black Labradors burst into the kitchen, causing Paddington to jump into Serena's arms in fright.

'Oh, bugger, sorry – didn't realise you had a cat,' said the painter. 'Shall I put them back in the van?'

'No, no, it's fine. I'll shut Paddington in the scullery,' said Serena, depositing her disgruntled feline into the unwelcoming lit-tle room when she'd so been enjoying the warmth of the Rayburn. 'Are these the twins?' Serena asked.

'Yes. My babies: Basil and Manuel,' said the decorator. Serena smiled at the blank looks coming from Pete and Ashna as they digested the dogs' names. Although he looked fairly young, the man must have been in his thirties to remember repeats of *Fawlty Towers*.

'And I'm Max,' he said, introducing himself to Serena and the others. 'Local painter and decorator. I promise you, no one is better or cheaper,' he announced confidently.

'Good to meet you. Come on,' Serena said. 'I'll show you what needs doing.'

Will disappeared into his study while Max followed Serena around the house, a notepad and stubby pencil in hand.

After concluding their tour, they returned to the kitchen where Pete and Ashna were making a great fuss of the dogs.

'Would you like a coffee?' asked Serena.

'Love one, please. Milk, no sugar,' Max replied, ripping a page from the notebook. 'Here's my quote, by the way. I'm not one to hang about. And don't be embarrassed if it sounds like too much. Just tell me the most important things and I can give you an instant re-quote.'

Serena put the kettle on, then took the page from Max and gulped. Heavens. She knew it was probably a snip, but it was still far more than they could afford.

'Um, well, if we were maybe to start with this, this and this,' she said, underlining a few tasks. 'What would that come to?' she asked.

Fortunately, the diocese had been in touch the day before to confirm they'd be preparing their five-yearly report on any works they considered essential in the house in the next few weeks so Serena was hoping the Church would be able to stump up for some of the jobs she'd now deferred. She was fairly sure they wouldn't mind who did them, so with any luck they'd be able to keep Max on. They'd even made noises about providing some funding for tidying up the overgrown garden.

Sensing the delicacy of the conversation, Ashna and Pete upped the volume of their dog-fussing. Serena smiled inwardly. Those two were always in cahoots and she couldn't have been more pleased. She just knew they'd be perfectly suited. Max consulted his pad again and wrote a revised figure at the bottom of the page. It was much more manageable as a starting point.

'When can you begin?' she asked.

'Soon as you like,' Max replied. 'And if you want, I could give you a quote for the garden at some stage too,' he added. 'I do landscaping as well as decorating.'

Serena was about to reply when Pete chipped in.

'No need for that, mate. I've got it covered,' he said. 'Serena, could I have a word?'

They made their way out of the back door to the garden.

'Is everything okay?' Serena asked Pete.

'Yeah, 'course, but listen: I'm not payin' the goin' rate for rent and was hopin' to find a way to help out a bit more. Before I started gettin' into trouble, I did a course in landscape gardenin'. Least I can do is get the garden sorted for you,' he offered, his eyes twinkling. 'Come and have a quick look now and I'll tell you what I'm thinkin' . . .' he offered. Will popped his head out into the garden a moment later, then came out, as Pete was keen to discuss his provisional plans with the two of them.

Serena couldn't believe it. She'd always thought of Ashna as an angel sent from above, but she was starting to think she and Will had been sent two angels. Thank goodness, she thought, remembering Mrs Pipe's words on her birthday about the curse. With any luck, she thought, the good might just outweigh any darkness.

'I'm chilly,' said Serena after a couple of minutes outside. 'Let me just grab my coat.' She left the men chatting and went back into the kitchen and through to the scullery to find her parka. Max and Ashna were talking in the kitchen.

'I love your dogs,' Ashna was saying. 'I used to have a black lab. Briefly, anyway. Snoozy, I called him, as he loved a nap.'

'They're the best, aren't they?'

'Gorgeous. I found him – he'd been abandoned and I took him in, but my father had him put down.'

'Why?' asked Max, looking shocked.

'He'd been away on business and when he got back and found I'd taken in a stray dog, he was furious. Said he'd have fleas and all kinds of diseases. I begged him just to take the dog to the shelter, but he said he was doing the animal a favour. I couldn't stop him,' she explained.

'Of course not – he sounds like a beast. If there's one thing I can't stand, it's cruelty to animals . . . Sorry, I'm sure he's got his good points, but sheesh . . .' Max puffed out his cheeks, reeling from the story, shock and empathy in his eyes.

'No need to apologise. He doesn't really. That's why I'm here . . .' Ashna began, explaining that she was new to the village.

'I only moved to Cattlebridge a few months ago too. I lived in Tunbridge Wells before – that's where my family's from. But when I started my painting and decorating course at a college in Hastings, I wanted to move a bit nearer. Always fancied living in a village and the cottage I'm renting on the high street is lovely. Tiny, but fine for just me. Well, me and the dogs. There's a little garden, so it's perfect.'

'It sounds lovely,' smiled Ashna.

'Not too shabby, especially now I've used all my newly acquired painting skills on it! Now, tell me more about you. How did you end up in the village?'

Ashna gave him a summary of what had led her to the Vicarage before turning the questions back to him.

'Why did you want to leave the town you're from? Was it just so you'd be nearer to college or was there something else?' she asked.

A cloud passed over Max's face and his cheerful smile vanished. But before he could answer, Serena disturbed them, having finally located her coat under a mound of other jackets.

'Max is new to the village, just like the rest of us,' Ashna explained to Serena, embarrassed she might have hit a nerve with her questions and gabbling to cover her concern.

'No way!' Serena replied. 'A place for new beginnings – starting with this house, thank goodness. Max, I can hardly wait for you to begin!'

12.
JULY–AUGUST 1998

It had been two years since Serena had stayed with Freddie in Majorca and, although there had been no romance between them then or indeed any indication of it in their letters since, Serena had developed an unwavering crush. She was eighteen now and had just finished her A Levels when she received a beautiful wedding invitation in the post. Amber, one of Freddie's sisters, was getting married in Majorca in August and, unbelievably, had invited Serena to the wedding. Her immediate thought was that Luna would be put out she hadn't been included on the invitation, but then she remembered her sister was going to Greece with a friend and wasn't due back until the day of the wedding. Enclosed with the stiff cream card was a scribbled note from Freddie:

'Please come! I was allowed to invite a "plus one" and couldn't think of anyone I'd love to have as a partner more than you. The invitation looks posh but the wedding won't be conventional – Amber's going to be barefoot with daisies in her hair. Let me know if you can make it. You're welcome to come and stay for as long as you want. I'm on my gap year still and not yet off on any travels. Love Freddie x'

For the second time in only a few moments, Serena was astonished. *'Love Freddie x'* was the most affectionate sign-off she'd ever received from him. He normally just wrote '*Freddie*' – plain and simple. Serena's heart began to dance with hope. Maybe, just maybe, this year would be different.

༄

Serena emerged from the stiflingly hot Arrivals hall and peered around, hoping she'd still recognise her pen pal. She knew she hadn't changed much herself. She was a little taller and slimmer now, perhaps, but her curly hair remained long and blonde, her face round and unadorned with make-up.

'Serena!' came a shout and all of a sudden he was there. Freddie. Immediately, he gathered Serena into a hug and lifted her up, spinning her round and round. She laughed, expecting him to find her heavy and put her down, but he didn't. He carried on spinning her, oblivious to the crowds around them, and Serena stopped worrying about her weight or anyone else and tipped her head back, dizzy and joyful.

Eventually Freddie released her and took charge of the luggage trolley and they made their way out of the hall into the evening sunshine, gabbling away to each other as comfortable old friends always do. But as familiar as he was to her, Serena knew their friendship was no longer enough. In the car she studied him, observing his beautiful profile, trying to work out if he might have feelings to match her own. She had no idea if Freddie's remarkable greeting was a sign of deeper feelings for her or simply an expression of his boundless, reckless energy.

An hour later, they had wound their way up to Deia, but instead of taking the turning to the farmhouse, the rusty old car took a left down towards the beach – Cala Deia. Freddie parked in the shade of some trees.

'Come on then,' he said. 'Thought you might like to see the beach again before we head home. It's total wedding chaos there and everyone will want your advice on what to wear.'

'I doubt it,' said Serena, smiling. She was not generally anyone's sartorial muse. But she was happy with the turn of events. It was dusk. That wonderful time of day when holidaymakers traipsed up the hill from the beach, weary from roasting themselves all day long, but evening diners heading to Ca's Patro March, the beachside seafood restaurant, had yet to arrive. It was quiet. The sun was low in the sky. They made it down to the beach and had settled themselves on some rocks when Freddie turned Serena towards him by gently tugging her hair. He kissed her.

'I can't believe it!' Serena said, as they drew apart after a while. 'I've fancied you forever,' she told Freddie honestly. 'But I thought it was one-sided.'

'You're kidding me,' said Freddie, as he pulled Serena back towards him. 'Serena, you're blind. I've been in love with you since the first moment I met you. I remember you straightening your hair that time and I hated it because your curls are just so much a part of you. But I didn't want to take advantage. I know you're only a year younger than me, but it just felt wrong before. I was seriously tempted on a couple of occasions though, and you know what I'm like, I don't usually think before I act. I think I just cared about you too much to do anything rash. But, Serena, you're eighteen now. I don't think anyone could call me dishonourable for letting my true feelings out at last.'

The days that followed were the happiest Serena had ever known. The farmhouse was abuzz with preparations for the wedding and, with so much going on, Freddie and Serena were able to come and go as they pleased. They spent long days at the beach sunning themselves and racing each other in the sea before heading back to the *finca* for late dinners with the family, then heading out to bars and finally tumbling into bed together in the early hours of the morning. Freddie's mother Bobbi was truly bohemian and had no issue with Serena sharing a room with Freddie. She welcomed her back into the family as if she were another daughter.

Malcolm too was easy company and several magical evenings were spent sitting around a camp fire while he played retro tunes on his guitar, singing along with his gravelly voice to 'Hotel California', 'House of the Rising Sun' and Eric Clapton's 'Layla', songs Serena would forever associate with those blissful, balmy evenings spent in such relaxed and loving company, Freddie's arms around her as he buried his face in her hair.

One day, Serena borrowed Ebony's bike and she and Freddie cycled up and down winding, precipitous roads and then off the beaten track, Serena determined to keep up with Freddie's pace. By the time they reached the secluded café Freddie had in mind, she was beetroot-coloured and gasping for a drink. The café was seemingly in the middle of nowhere, although there were a few locals enjoying a drink, and it overlooked a stunning bay, equally hidden from the tourist trade. They seated themselves at a small plastic table with the best view and Serena ordered a Sprite. Never had a fizzy drink felt so refreshing. She wafted a menu in front of her face to try to cool it down and ignored the wobbly-jelly feeling in her thighs.

'You just need a dip,' Freddie said. 'That'll cool you down. We can climb down to the beach from here as soon as we've had some lunch.'

'Perfect,' Serena said. And it was. They enjoyed a meal that was as delicious as it was simple: grilled fish, served with a fresh green salad. They chatted comfortably, Serena full of questions about Freddie's family, who intrigued her no end. They were all such characters, aside from Little Jane, who was sweet and shy.

'Tell me,' said Serena, taking another gulp of her drink. 'Why is Little Jane called Jane when the rest of you have more unusual names? I've been wondering about it.'

'Ah, well, she's named after my mum's sister. She died when Mum was expecting Jane. Mum was devastated about it, so she decided to name the baby after her. And, of course, Jane has always been teeny – just like our aunt – so she quickly became Little Jane.'

'How sad,' said Serena, frowning. 'Puzzle solved, anyway. I love your family so much,' she told him. 'It feels like being gripped in a huge, warm hug being here with you all. You're so lucky.'

'I guess so, though it can be pretty intimidating having three sisters sometimes! How about your family? What are they like?'

'Dad is reserved, but very warm and lovely. Mum is sweet, though she can be quite distant. She's always ridiculously bothered about what people think. And my twin sister is . . . a handful, I guess you could call her. We're complete opposites, even though we're twins.'

'Really? I imagined you'd be identical.'

'We are, to look at. But not as characters. Anyway, hopefully you'll meet them all at some point. Blimey, the sun's really heating up now, isn't it? Shall we go for that swim?'

'Sure, let me just pay the bill and we'll go. You can make a start, if you want. Just be careful on the rocks.'

Serena edged down the rocks carefully, wondering where Freddie had got to. He was taking ages paying the bill. She reached the sandy cove below and looked up, expecting to see Freddie clambering down behind her. Instead, she saw he was standing dangerously close to the edge of the cliff above – not far from where they'd just enjoyed their lunch.

'Freddie, what are you doing?' she shouted up. She was starting to feel panicky. It made her feel a bit dizzy even looking at him. Her heart began to hammer.

'Watch this!' Freddie shouted from above and he jumped, his hands by his sides as he plunged into the sea. It must have been a drop of at least thirty feet. Serena waited in horror, hoping desperately Freddie would emerge. It seemed to take forever; she was almost in tears.

But eventually he shot up out of the water like a firework, whooping and hollering. He swam neatly through the waves and ran up the beach to Serena.

'What the hell were you doing?' Serena shouted. She was like a mother scolding a child who's almost run under a bus. 'You could have killed yourself!'

'Hey, chill, Serena. It's okay. I've done it before.'

'But there must be rocks. It's such a height. Freddie, you scared the life out of me.'

'I'm sorry . . . It was stupid of me,' he said, immediately contrite. 'I was showing off. I didn't stop and think that you'd be worried. Forgive me?' he asked, his puppy-dog eyes beseeching her. Serena nodded, calmer now, and she was distracted soon enough as Freddie began to kiss her.

The next couple of hours were spent in the sea and, out of view of the café, making love on the beach with a new intensity that seemed to have been born of their first mild disagreement. And it really was love they made, Serena drinking in the scent of Freddie's skin. He always seemed to smell of summer.

'Tomorrow I'm taking you shopping,' Freddie said as he shifted his position on the sand.

'Really? What kind of shopping?' Serena asked. She didn't like to tell him she loathed shopping for clothes. She did like buying trinkets and treasures though, and she'd spotted some lovely shops that might sell just those kinds of things in Deia.

'For a ring.'

Serena laughed. 'A ring?' she repeated.

'Uh-huh. Look, you'll think I'm crazy and I know I can be impulsive, but what about if we got married? Okay, maybe not right away,' he added, as he clocked the mild alarm on Serena's face. 'But in a year, maybe? I know we're young but, shit, I'm crazy about you, Serena, and I love the idea of getting married young, having loads of babies . . . What do you think?'

Serena felt a bit sick with panic – not because she didn't feel the same, but at the thought of explaining a teenage marriage to her parents, although she supposed she wouldn't be far off twenty in a year's time. A million questions ran through her mind.

'I'd love to,' Serena told him honestly. 'But what about our plans for university? And where would we live? And what about our parents?'

'Such a stickler for practicalities,' Freddie teased. 'I don't know the answers yet but we'll sort it all out. All I know is that I'd like to return to Majorca after university. Could you bear that?'

'That pretty much clinches the deal, regardless of my boring old practicalities. I absolutely love it here,' Serena told him, smiling.

The very next day, Freddie bought her a ring. Not an engagement ring as such – an eternity ring of sorts from a charming bohemian jeweller's up the hill, near the ancient church of San Juan.

'Us, always,' Freddie whispered as he pushed the ring onto Serena's index finger. They were watching the sun set over the olive groves and Serena felt a lump in her throat.

She was floating in a bubble of bliss, too happy to even worry that it might eventually burst.

Having enjoyed nearly a month in Majorca, Serena had stupidly booked to return to England the day after Amber's wedding.

She hadn't thought it through – she should have booked for the following day – but her flight wasn't changeable. Still, she wasn't going to let an early start deter her from enjoying herself.

And Amber's wedding day was the most exquisite occasion from start to finish. The ceremony took place in the garden, right beside the orchard, where an array of beautifully coloured rugs had been scattered around for guests to sit on. Amber had decided she didn't want to be given away so she arrived in the garden wearing a wispy cream dress made exclusively of lace and with a crown of daisies on her head. When she sashayed along the aisle of grass, Dan, her soon-to-be husband, ran towards her and whisked her into his arms. It was the most romantic thing Serena had ever seen and it seemed to affect all the guests – she'd never seen so many love-struck couples before. And as for her and Freddie, they were inseparable all night. Serena's flight the next morning was at ten o'clock and they decided that to sleep was to waste time.

'We'll sleep when we're dead,' said Freddie, quoting his favourite heavy metal band. Every moment of life was to be seized, as far as Freddie was concerned. They arrived at Palma airport at eight, almost delirious with tiredness and, as Serena checked in, she thought Freddie must literally be delirious when he suddenly decided to buy a last-minute ticket to London and accompany Serena home.

'Why not?' he said, his delicious dark eyes red-rimmed but more gorgeous than ever. 'I've got my passport – I always have it on me for ID. There's nowhere else I'd rather be than with you,' he smiled, peeling notes from his wallet to pay for his ticket. Serena was incredibly flattered, knowing how hard Freddie had been working at various bars to earn that cash. But the relaxed persona she'd taken on in Majorca was starting to fade even before they'd landed in London. Bobbi and Malcolm may have been wonderfully bohemian, but her own parents were not and she was anxious Freddie would find her life abysmally dull and bourgeois compared to his Majorcan lifestyle, especially as they would have to sleep in separate rooms.

She needn't have worried. Her mother was charmed by Freddie's manners and good looks, her father was a quiet yet welcoming host, and Luna – well, Luna was the most charming of all.

13.
APRIL 2015

By Easter, the house had definitely turned a corner, Serena decided, as she stretched her aching back and surveyed the newly transformed garden. For one thing, as winter turned gently into spring, the house was warmer, especially as they kept the log burners roaring. For another, she and Pete had been grafting away in the garden for weeks and the exercise had transformed her – she was sleeping well and there was even some colour in her cheeks again. Serena could hardly believe how Pete's clever layout (and back-breaking labour) had turned the enormous space from an overgrown field into a beautiful landscape divided into four sections. A large patio was now accessible from the kitchen, filled with terracotta pots brimming with spring flowers including pretty primroses and vibrant crocuses, and brick steps led up to a lawn with raised borders on either side. Here, an array of scented and variously coloured roses had been planted and Ashna enjoyed practising her yoga and meditation on the grass, beside an old apple tree. A newly clipped hedge crossed the middle of the lawn and an archway through it led to an open meadow. Currently, only the wild grasses were evident, with a path mown through them, but they'd scattered a selection of seeds and Pete had assured Serena that, by summer, the meadow would be bursting with wild flowers.

Pete had surprised them all with his incredible knowledge of horticulture. He was an expert on the famous gardener Gertrude Jekyll, and passionate about gardens, most particularly wild ones. Serena now knew all about the African daisies, baby blue eyes, dog violets, yellow celandines, bluebells and cornflowers that would emerge before they knew it.

At the far end of the garden, beyond the meadow, was an area that was now given over to a large vegetable patch. It was this that had become Serena's domain and she was thoroughly enjoying reading up on what to plant that was seasonal. Will was the cook in their household – he'd always been an excellent chef – but it was wonderful to think she'd soon be able to contribute something to their suppers.

It was now Good Friday and almost time for the sombre midday service. As always seemed to happen on this particular bank holiday, the sky had clouded over as the clock hands edged closer towards the moment of the crucifixion.

'You guys had better finish up soon,' Serena said to Ashna and Max, who were both in downward dog poses on the lawn. 'Think it's going to chuck it down before long.'

'I've been telling her that for the last ten minutes,' Max muttered. 'We're going to get soaked any minute. There, I felt a drop of rain. And Pete's going to help me fix my van before lunch. I can't keep him waiting . . .'

'Don't you dare move,' Ashna scolded him. 'Such a bad student. You were the one who told me your neck was hurting. I can help you, but not if you keep making excuses! Now, breathe!'

Serena laughed to herself. She'd never heard Ashna being so strict. She hurried inside to change for the service, swapping her gardening clothes for a long black skirt and a silver top, adding jingling silver bangles and the beautiful sea-green scarf Ashna had given her. She dabbed on a little lip gloss and dashed into the study, where she found Will putting the final touches to his sermon.

'You look beautiful,' Will said, looking up at Serena and putting his papers away.

'Thank you, my darling, but come on,' she said. 'The vicar can't be late!'

'True,' he laughed. 'But then again, they can't start without me.' Serena smiled at his oft-used joke.

The service that followed was mournful, 'There is a Green Hill Far Away' and 'My Song is Love Unknown' sending shivers down Serena's spine as they always did. She would be glad to get to Easter Day and a more joyful service. She closed her eyes, endeavouring to shut out all thoughts at the same time, and was relieved to return home to the fish pie Ashna had warmed through for the four of them in the Rayburn.

'How was the service?' asked Pete, helping himself to a hearty portion while Serena sloshed white wine into all four glasses. Will and Serena had briefly contemplated giving up wine for Lent, but had opted for chocolate in the end. Maybe next year . . .

'Good, thanks,' answered Will. 'Easter's always lovely – the contrast between serious Good Friday and joyful Easter Sunday. Holy Sunday, Mrs Pipe still calls it. I know the congregation are all still comparing me to the last chap, but at least the younger ones seem happy enough with me. It's the oldies that are the toughies,' he said, grinning good-naturedly.

'Sorry I couldn't make it today, mate. I promised Max I'd help him fix his van,' explained Pete. 'But I'll be there Easter Sunday, I promise.'

'No pressure, old chap. Whatever you like. It's not part of the deal, just because you're living in a vicarage.'

'I know, but I promised the prison chaplain I'd go to church once a month and I'm gonna stick to my word. Call it part of my rehabilitation . . .'

They were halfway through the meal when the telephone rang.

'I'll get it,' said Will, scraping back his chair. He raced up to the freshly painted hall where an old-fashioned telephone sat trilling loudly into the echoing space.

'Vicarage,' sang Will as he pushed back his hair and crouched down next to the hall table.

'Afternoon,' came the barked response. 'Colonel Feltham-Jones here. One arm,' he clarified, which nearly made Will snort with laughter. The Colonel was distinctive enough to remember without him needing to describe his lack of limb, but it was clearly how he liked to introduce himself.

'How can I help, Colonel?' asked Will.

'Was speaking to Miss Dawson yesterday. She told me you and your lady friend play the piano. Correct?' he bellowed.

'Er, yes, that's right. Or at least we used to. We don't have a piano at the moment.'

'Reason I'm calling, old chap. Got a piano here if you'd like it. Belonged to my wife. No use for it now.' The Colonel's wife had died only recently and, while he put on a great show of resilience, Will was certain he was sad and lonely underneath. 'You'll just need to pick it up.'

'Fantastic,' enthused Will. He was always keen to receive any offers of charity – it was a necessity with a salary as pathetic as his – and the house still felt bare and in need of more furnishings. As well, it would be lovely to play again and perhaps it would be good for Serena too. He finished off making arrangements with the Colonel before telling the others the good news.

'Reminds me of something that happened at the prison,' Pete said, topping up everyone's wine glasses. 'Some kind, deluded soul like the old Colonel donated a piano to the jail one day but the screws didn't really know where to put it, so for a while it was just outside my cell. Nobody was usin' it, but one of the guards used to rest up against it when he was on duty at night and fancied a little snooze. Then me and my cellmate Paddy had an idea – lovely Irish lad he was, probably not really called Paddy, but that's your name if you're servin' time and you're Irish.' Will chuckled at this.

'Anyway, one evenin' Paddy fed this dozy guard some ghost story about a house he'd lived in once what was haunted – he could tell a good tale could Paddy, and he really went to town. All about this ghost playin' the piano in the middle of the night. So that night the screw's just settlin' down for a little nap around midnight when Paddy gets out a phone he's had smuggled into the prison. He's found a bit of piano music on there, so he turns it up super loud and starts playin'. Some dramatic tune or other. We've got a great view of the guard from the cell window and we see his eyes open, then he goes rigid with fear. He takes one look at the piano, sees there's no one playin' it, and just legs it down the corridor. Screamin' like a baby he was. Poor sod. Bit cruel of us, I s'pose, but it gets a bit dull sometimes inside. You live for a little joke or two.'

'What happened to him? The guard?' asked Serena, laughing.

'They moved him down to the other wing. Knew he'd just be baited by us lot after that. They shifted the piano too. Never did know where it ended up.'

'Well, I'm sure this piano will have a far less eventful life,' Will said, smiling. 'Actually, you wouldn't be able to help me move it, would you, Pete?'

''Course I could. Just don't expect me to play it, that's all.'

The following evening, on Easter Saturday, Will and Pete arrived at the Black Horse to meet Max and local farmer Jake Hardy, who'd both agreed to help them move the piano from the Colonel's house to the Vicarage. Will hadn't met Jake before, but he and the Colonel appeared to be firm friends and had arranged for the piano to be transported on a trailer hooked up to Jake's tractor.

'You must be Jake!' Will said, clapping the farmer on the back and offering him a drink before they set off.

'Kind of you,' replied Jake with quiet reserve. 'But I don't drink. Been on the wagon for a couple of years now. Whisky got the better of me, but the Colonel's wife helped me. I'm that sad she's passed away,' he muttered into his scraggy, sandy beard that matched his scraggy, sandy hair.

'Shouldn't be in the pub should you, Jakey!' came a loud female voice from the corner of the inn. Will searched around and was surprised to see a buxom woman emerge from the shadows. She was clad from head to toe in leopard print, her cleavage was out of this world and her pouty lips were painted cerise pink.

'Going to introduce me then?' she asked Jake, daintily flapping her bejewelled fingers in Will's direction.

'Er, yes, er, this is the new vicar, love,' Jake told her. 'Will, this is my wife, Tanya,' he managed, before sinking into his collar.

'Not your typical farmer's wife,' whispered Max, who'd ordered Will a pint of bitter and passed it over to him. Pete's mouth was open in an expression of horror as he assessed the predatory Tanya.

It transpired that Tanya worked in the pub and, while her quiet husband may have found sobriety, she apparently had no intention of joining him. As she cleared glasses from the tables she seemed to think it a perk of the job to finish any dregs left in them and every so often, when the beer bubbles became too much for her, she let out a loud belch. She was a triumph for the landlord, however, as she was very persuasive with her customers. After several pints, Will decided they really should get on with collecting the piano.

'Come on, lads,' he said, feeling decidedly merry. 'Time we were off.'

'Don't you gorgeous men be leaving me just yet,' admonished Tanya. 'Come on, one more for the road,' she said, pouring three pints without taking no for an answer and the men happily enjoyed another drink together before finally getting on their way with Jake, their designated tractor driver.

'Hop yourselves into the trailer,' he told them as he swung up into the cab and started the engine. The three lads jumped up, giddy now from the sudden burst of fresh air. Ten minutes later they arrived at the Colonel's house. He was at the door, beckoning them in immediately as he smoked his pipe.

'Where've you been? Got the sherry out and ready for you hours ago. Some crisps too. They'll be stale soon. Come on! Come along in,' he bellowed, waving his one arm around expansively. The Colonel's house was a beautiful property, there was no doubt, and it was cosily furnished with antiques and ancient rugs. It was clear though that it was lacking a woman's touch. In the sitting room a fire was roaring in the hearth, but, rather than lamplight, an overly bright ceiling light illuminated the room and there were piles of books and *Country Life* magazines strewn around. The room smelt strongly of pipe tobacco and when Will sat down on the sofa, narrowly avoiding squashing the Colonel's spectacles, he could see through to the kitchen where the sink was brimming with unwashed crockery and pans. His heart went out to the old fellow and he knew he couldn't possibly leave before partaking in at least a couple of drinks. He hoped Serena wouldn't wait up for him.

Serena yawned and stretched out in the bed. It seemed too large without Will beside her and she checked her bedside clock again. It was past midnight and there was no sign of him, which wasn't unusual for Will, who tended to lose track of time in the pub, but she was surprised he was enjoying a bender the night before Easter Sunday. He'd regret it in the morning, but there was no point in Serena staying awake too. She took off her reading glasses, put down her book and turned out the light, pulling the thick duvet tight around her.

The next thing she knew she was awake, her heart thudding heavily in her chest. She felt beside her. Still no Will. She strained her ears, listening out for whatever had woken her. *Nothing,* she thought and was just about to turn over when she heard a noise. She jumped out of bed and crept to the bedroom door, which creaked disconcertingly as she opened it. She stepped out onto the landing and made her way stealthily along the corridor. And then she stopped dead still. It was that noise again and this time there was no question what it was. The wail of a baby. She felt the hairs on the back of her neck stand up and gripped hold of the newly polished banister. *Where's it coming from?* she asked herself, panicky now. She made her way a little further along the landing and all at once the noise grew louder. The nursery. Her heart was now in her throat as she crept up to the door and swung it open.

'Paddington!' she cried. 'What are you doing in here? You silly thing, getting stuck.'

The mewling of the cat. Not a baby after all. Serena took some deep breaths and bundled Paddington into her arms, taking her through to the bedroom. She placed her in Will's spot and lay in the bed listening to her heart reverberate in her ribcage. The sensible side of her knew it was just a case of Paddington getting stuck in the nursery, but deep within her she felt a sense of misgiving. There was something about that room that wasn't right. She shuddered and curled herself into the foetal position. Eventually she drifted off until she was disturbed by Will climbing into bed in the early hours. She pulled him to her, ignoring the alcohol fumes – just glad to have him home again.

14.
AUGUST 1998

Freddie's impromptu stay with Serena was a surprising success, at least to start with. Serena had been in such a panic that life in her small village in rural England would fail to match up to bohemian Deia, but Freddie seemed more than happy to fit into a different kind of life with the Meadows. The village was not particularly beautiful, and it certainly wasn't buzzing, but it had a certain sleepy charm to it. It was inland but only a short drive to the sea on the South East coast and, while Serena's own house was an uninspiring 1960s semi in a quiet close, there were quaint Tudor cottages dotted around, a pleasant park and a couple of pubs. At the Rose and Crown Serena introduced Freddie to her and Luna's friends and they hung around playing pool, listening to the Manic Street Preachers on the jukebox while they drank bottles of lager. On brighter days, the group lounged lazily in the beer garden, playing card games and enjoying that wonderful gift of time to squander, available only to the very young.

Freddie was a hit with everyone. The girls giggled and flicked their hair when he teased them and the boys thought him the absolute essence of cool and started squeezing lemon into their hair in an attempt to bring out the natural highlights (largely unsuccessfully).

He seemed to enhance Serena's own popularity too, as if she'd passed some kind of test by introducing her heavenly boyfriend to the gang. She'd always been in Luna's shadow until now and suddenly she was the twin the telephone rang for as plans were made for trips to the beach or outings on the train to Hastings or Tunbridge Wells for shopping and yet more hanging around. Serena, in these moments, found herself less pleased than anxious. She watched Luna's face as the days progressed, the charming smiles her sister had been ready with at the start of the week becoming more forced – her eyes betraying her real feelings, only visible to Serena. Luna's thunder had been stolen. And she didn't like it.

She began an attack – Freddie the unknowing victim – but Serena was blindly confident in their love for one another. Serena almost pitied her as Luna joined the couple on the sofa to watch *Trainspotting* for the umpteenth time, snuggling up on the other side of Freddie. Serena felt Freddie move imperceptibly towards her and smiled to herself. Luna would not give up though. She was brazen. On the beach, she wore skimpier and skimpier bikinis (Serena in her trusty old navy swimsuit); in the pub, she would somehow always make sure she was sitting next to Freddie, where she would take the liberty of trying out whatever he was drinking.

In the end, Serena and Freddie laughed about it.

'My sister fancies you,' Serena said one evening when they'd managed to extricate themselves from Luna for long enough to go for a walk to the park alone. Serena sat on a swing and Freddie took the one next to her, his long legs stretched out in front of him.

'I know, she's pretty obvious. It's amazing how identical-looking you are, but how different you are otherwise. There's something unsettling about her,' Freddie said, frowning, and Serena felt reassured. It was clear to her that Luna didn't stand a chance.

Freddie had been with them for ten days when Serena was asked to babysit for the vicar's children one evening. She asked if Freddie could go with her, but the vicar was very strait-laced and made it clear she should come alone.

'Do you mind?' Serena asked Freddie. 'It's just one evening, and I could use the cash. I'll be back by eleven.'

''Course not.'

'Mum and Dad are out tonight and Luna said she might be going out too, so I'm afraid you'll probably be all alone.'

'I'll survive,' he said, laughter in his eyes. 'I'll watch *EastEnders* and pine for you to get back.'

They kissed and Serena left him opening a can of beer in the kitchen.

She got home earlier than expected. The vicar's wife had been suffering with a bad headache and they'd returned by half past nine. Serena had stuffed her cash in her purse and hurried home. There was no sign of Freddie, but she heard music coming from Luna's room – her favourite, Massive Attack.

The door was slightly ajar. She pushed it open. Then she froze. She wanted to cover her eyes with her hands, or run away – far, far away – but it was as though she was glued to the floor. And the worst thing was that they didn't realise she was there and so the scene was not one of shocked faces and pulled-up bed sheets, but instead an image of entwined, mobile bodies. Legs wrapped around each other, Luna's bare back, Freddie's strong arms. Serena snapped.

'What the hell are you doing?' she yelled, her voice high and strangled.

It was the ultimate betrayal and the aftermath felt dirty and messy. Freddie was full of remorse and weak explanations about

Luna's powers of persuasion and his own impulsive and fallible nature. He begged for forgiveness.

Luna behaved as if nothing untoward had happened at all. As if Serena were making a great fuss about nothing. Serena found this attitude possibly the most galling thing of all. The fact that, to Luna, it had meant nothing to lure Serena's boyfriend into bed with her. It had been merely a point to score.

The day after it happened was the day of the twins' A Level results. Stephanie drove them to their sixth-form college, Freddie having taken a train to London to stay with an old school friend, his tail between his legs. The girls were keeping the sordid episode to themselves, in unspoken agreement, and Stephanie put their odd behaviour down to nerves, although she was confused when their mood failed to be enhanced by their both receiving the grades they needed (Luna pipping Serena at the post, with one more 'A' grade). Their mother was glowing in their reflected glory, as the girls won places at the University of Surrey, where they'd both been planning to study: Serena midwifery, Luna media studies with English literature.

But if there was one thing Serena now knew, it was that she could no longer be a part of Luna's life. Secretly, telling no one, she went through clearing and managed to secure herself a place at a college in Sheffield, as far away from Luna as possible. She wasn't able to get onto another midwifery course, so she opted for another of her strengths – languages – instead. She told her parents she'd had a change of mind about career direction and that the new university she'd chosen was renowned for its French and Spanish courses.

She could see her mother wavering when she announced her decision. Serena could tell she was trying to assess what people would think. She'd already told everyone that Serena was going to train as a midwife, but then again languages did sound a bit more *academic*. Her friend Sheila's son was going to study French and she was always going on about how clever he was. Yes, Stephanie would look forward to telling her at book club. She smiled, and Serena was relieved. Arthur was more concerned.

'But you've always wanted to be a midwife!' he said.

'I've changed my mind,' Serena told him, definite.

'Well, as long as you're sure . . .' he said, squeezing her hand.

She was. It was over with Freddie, and with Luna too. Serena had decided she was better off alone.

15.
APRIL 2015

The next thing Will knew, it was Easter Sunday and he had a raging hangover.

'Good night?' asked Serena as she brought him a cup of tea. She'd decided not to tell Will about her shock in the night. In the cold light of day, it seemed silly. Just a cat stuck in a bedroom after all, and perhaps a worrying indication of the state of her subconscious. Will groaned and buried his red thatch of hair in the pillow.

'What on earth happened?' asked Serena. 'Where's the piano?'

Will groaned again. 'I have a feeling it may be outside the front door,' he admitted. Serena pulled back the curtains – beautiful pale blue drapes with embroidered flowers along the hem, recently made and hung by Ashna. Will's eyes protested at the sparkling morning light.

'Yep, there it is,' confirmed Serena. 'Some of the local kids are playing it now. What happened?'

'Long story, but let's just say it involved far too much alcohol and I treated the neighbourhood to some of my favourite tunes on the piano as Jake drove us home from the Colonel's. We were in the trailer attached to his tractor. Max and Pete accompanied me with some pretty raucous singing,' he chuckled ruefully. 'Lord knows who saw us. We got the piano to the front door but we were far too drunk to manage to get it inside, so I had the good idea of leaving it outdoors. I hope it didn't rain. Will the diocese sack me, do you think?' asked Will, pulling Serena down onto the bed and kissing her on the lips.

'Yuck, hangover kiss,' she laughed. 'And they won't sack you if they don't find out, which, unless Miss Dawson saw you, they probably won't. You'll definitely be fired if you miss the service though,' she teased, checking her watch. 'You've only got half an hour.'

'Bollocks,' Will cursed as he jumped out of bed and raced, naked, into the en suite to shower. 'There's no hot water again!' he yelped a moment later.

'Boiler's playing up,' Serena replied with a sigh. 'Will we ever get this place sorted?' she asked, holding out a towel for a freezing Will to wrap himself in as he hopped out of the shower.

'We will, for sure. You've done amazingly well so far. The place looks much homelier now. We just need more furniture. At least we've got a piano,' he said, grinning broadly. Serena laughed. Will was a reprobate sometimes. But a lovable one.

After Will and Pete heaved the piano into the entrance hall, they made it to church in time – just – and Will managed to rise to the occasion despite his hangover. A packed house was a rarity in this day and age and Will wanted to make a good impression on his first Easter Sunday. During communion, he was interested to observe those parishioners who lingered a little longer than was usual at the altar. He would never have commented to anyone else on such observations, but it always gave him a clue as to those in his parish who might need his help. The Colonel was on his knees a little while, no doubt reflecting on his dearly missed wife. *I must visit him again soon*, thought Will. An elderly lady who helped with the flowers tarried too, and he made a mental note to ask after her. The surprise though was Alice Charles – the doctor's wife who'd attended Serena's birthday lunch. She was at the altar far longer than most, clearly deep in thought, her eyes fixed on the stained-glass window beyond with an expression of melancholy. He would drop in on her this week.

In the event though, Serena beat Will to it. On Tuesday morning, she was in the local chemist's, searching for her particular brand of curl-friendly shampoo, when she bumped – literally – into Alice, who as a result dropped the item she was holding. Serena knelt down to retrieve it for her, apologising profusely, only to note it was a pregnancy test. Her cheeks flamed red.

'Oh, I'm so sorry,' she said, handing back the test. It seemed to be the final straw for Alice and she burst instantly into tears. Serena discreetly took the test from her, paying for it and the shampoo, before returning to Alice.

'Come on,' she said and led Alice back to the Vicarage.

'Do you want to talk about it?' asked Serena, handing Alice a steaming mug of sweet tea. She'd been thankful to discover the kitchen empty of any of the other Vicarage residents, aside from Paddington, who was curled up next to the Rayburn. She and Alice were now sitting on either side of the pine table while Radio Four rumbled on at low volume in the background. The fridge hummed, the Rayburn oozed warmth, the newly transformed work table gleamed. All was tranquil.

'I don't even know why I got that damned test,' Alice said, brittle with tension. 'I know what the wretched result is.'

'And not the result you want?'

'No, absolutely not. It's going to be positive.'

Serena laid a hand tentatively on Alice's own. 'And that's bad?' she asked with a smile. 'I can't imagine something positive like that ever being negative,' she told her, gently.

'Well, that goes to show that you know nothing about my life,' snapped Alice and her eyes reddened again as she fought back fresh tears.

'So tell me,' said Serena, unfazed.

'I know what you think of me, what everyone thinks. There she goes, the ice queen, all she cares about are her nails and tennis and that snobby prep school she sends her children to. No warmth to her at all, no wonder he has to look elsewhere.'

'Rob?' asked Serena, shocked.

'Yes,' sighed Alice, the fight in her now vanished – she was like a damp pavement after a downpour of torrential rain. 'You've heard about his affairs, have you?'

'Not at all . . . Just from what you've said right now. And more than one?'

'Oh, yes,' said Alice, laughing bitterly. 'Many more than one, but this one takes the biscuit. It makes a mockery of me. Before, they've been nurses at the hospital, at least not right under my nose, but this one . . . I found out last night . . . It's that slut Tanya from the pub. Married to Jake Hardy.'

Good Lord, thought Serena. She'd met Tanya only yesterday at the Black Horse and she was definitely the sort of woman to leave an impression.

'Do you know for sure?' she asked.

'Oh, yes, he admits everything to me once I've found out. Then he swears he's a changed person. But this time . . . well, I just know I'm pregnant . . .' Alice wailed.

'Did you want to be pregnant?' asked Serena, her heart now hammering. 'Did you plan it?'

'Good heavens, no,' said Alice. 'Does anyone plan a third? But I've been pretty sure for the last week or so and I decided it was a good thing. A fresh start for us. Babies are wonderful at creating new beginnings, aren't they?'

Serena nodded, struggling to maintain her own composure now. But this wasn't about her. She pulled herself together.

'What will you do?' she asked and Alice shook her perfect coppery head.

'I don't know,' she said. 'I simply don't know.'

༺∽༻

Serena next saw Alice a fortnight later. The doorbell rang in the late morning as Serena was cleaning her hands in one of the sinks in the scullery after a session in the garden. She dried them and hurried to the door.

'I lost the baby,' were Alice's first words and Serena's heart crumpled for her.

Pete was in the kitchen, making tea in his overalls, having been roped into helping with the painting by Max, so Serena took Alice through to the drawing room. She'd forgotten that this was where all the industry was taking place until they came upon Max and Ashna (who Max had also persuaded to assist with the decorating). They had the radio on and when they saw Serena enter the room, they immediately asked her to settle an argument.

'Who sang this song? "House of the Rising Sun"?' asked Max. Serena wasn't really concentrating, aware that Alice needed to talk, but the answer popped into her head instantly.

'The Animals,' she answered.

'There, I told you,' giggled Ashna. 'Max thought it was The Eagles . . .'

Max pulled a face. 'Did you need me?' he asked Serena.

'No, sorry, I forgot you'd made a start on this room. It's okay, we'll use the study.'

The study was – mercifully – vacant. The log burner was roaring and all felt warm and snug. Serena and Alice sat at either end of a sofa.

'I'm so sorry to burden you with this,' said Alice. 'But you're the only person who knows I was pregnant. I took the test after I left here, and it was positive. I didn't know what to think or feel. I just felt numb. And that's the worst. I feel so guilty now that I wasn't elated about it. Like it's a punishment.'

She looked at Serena, her pale blue eyes mournful. 'I know I've no right to feel so grief-stricken about it all, but I do,' she cried. 'Serena, I feel so dreadfully sad.'

Serena took a deep breath. 'I lost a baby once too, you know,' she said. There, it was out, like an exhalation.

Serena paused for a moment, then added, 'I know just how you feel.'

16.

DECEMBER 2000

It proved easier than Serena had expected to cut herself off from Luna. In their first year at their respective universities, both girls threw themselves into the social life and, while Serena returned home for the holidays, Luna spent every opportunity travelling with her new friends – Interrailing through Europe, driving along the west coast of America, island-hopping around Greece. She earned well during term time, having taken numerous Student Union bar jobs, which helped to fund her wanderlust, and she was particularly skilled at making friends with the rich and well-to-do, such alliances providing cheap or free holidays in their salubrious vacation homes.

Towards the end of the second year, it was even easier to avoid her sister – Serena was studying languages and was lucky enough to spend a term at a university in Paris. She decided to stay on for longer too, taking a job as a waitress during the holidays to improve her French further. But she was now in the first term of her final year and dreading the Christmas holidays. For the first time in a long while, she'd be forced to spend time with Luna, who was bringing a new boyfriend home to meet the family. He was called Colin, and sounded ghastly. Serena herself was single, having ended a relationship with her French boyfriend when she left Paris. As lovely as he was, she couldn't be doing with long-distance relationships.

It was the last week of term and she'd been invited to a party. She was not in the mood. Her hair was all wrong and she had a tickle at the back of her throat, a sure sign a nasty cold was on its way. But she'd promised her best friend Lisa that she'd go along to give her moral support – there was an Aussie guy she had her eye on who was almost certainly going to be there. Serena knew him from her course and had been trying hard to get the two of them together for a while.

Serena searched half-heartedly through her wardrobe while Lisa applied make-up in the long mirror propped against the wall in Serena's room. The mirror reflected a typical student room – a single bed covered with an ethnic throw, burning joss sticks depositing fine grey ash all along the windowsill, a bamboo-style blind, a stereo pumping out Destiny's Child at high volume and clothes strewn on every available surface.

'Found anything?' asked Lisa, as she craned her neck to get in the right position to apply thick layers of mascara. She was already dressed in a black catsuit from Morgan and with her dark, poker-straight hair, pert bust and long legs she looked amazing, even if she would be freezing. Lisa was a hardy northerner and great fun, as well as an amazing listener. She wasn't afraid to call a spade a spade either, and was Serena's 'go-to' person for advice in times of crisis.

'Eurgh, I don't know. Maybe this?' asked Serena, as she held up a black shift dress.

'Too office-like,' said Lisa, dismissing Serena's effort and clambering up off the floor to search through the cupboard herself.

'Here,' she said, holding a red dress up against Serena.

'I don't remember this,' mused Serena. 'I don't think it's mine – is it yours?'

'Not mine. Must be Ellie's.' Ellie was the third occupant of their houseshare, but she had a long-term boyfriend and was usually at his place.

'It's gorgeous,' said Serena, her optimism for the evening increasing at the prospect of something decent to wear. The dress was figure hugging but, with long sleeves and a high neck, it wasn't too revealing and Serena wouldn't be cold even with just her thread-bare cord jacket thrown over the top. She tried it on. It fitted like a glove, the velvet material sensuous against her skin.

'Budge over,' she said to Lisa and she set to work on applying make-up, unusual for her.

'Flipping 'eck!' remarked Lisa ten minutes later. 'You look proper gorgeous. But your hair's not right.'

Serena sighed. The thing about curls was you never knew if they were going to behave or not.

'Here, let me try and put it up for you,' Lisa offered, and within minutes she'd managed to pile Serena's blonde curls on top of her head in a sophisticated topknot. 'We're going to knock 'em dead tonight,' said Lisa and they finished off their 'dressing vodkas' and headed out into the icy December dark.

❦

By the time they got there, the party was in full swing. Lisa immediately clocked the guy she was after and Serena started chatting to various faces she recognised from around the campus, although none of her circle of friends was there. These were the intellectuals, she recognised. The music was relaxed and, while loud, it was still possible to hear one another talk. Fashion was not high on the agenda and she realised she and Lisa were embarrassingly overdressed. Most of the crowd wore glasses and smoked pot. She made small talk with a group she knew from her course before heading into the kitchen to locate some alcohol. She found some warmish white wine and took a sip, blanching at the acidity as she swallowed it.

'Grim, isn't it?' said a man standing across the table from her. He was tall and his smile was dazzling – the teeth perfect and the grin wide. His eyes were dark blue, the skin around them already crinkling even in his early twenties, and his hair was thick and red. Serena took him in and found herself unable to respond. Her reaction was instant. She wanted him. It was that simple.

'You okay?' he asked, clearly alarmed at her muteness. She mentally shook herself.

'Yes, it's just . . .' Serena didn't know how to explain.

'I know,' the man said, grinning. 'I think I know. I feel it too. You're single?'

'Yes,' she said, slowly smiling.

'Then what are we waiting for? I'm Will,' he said and he took her hand. They found a quiet corner of the sitting room where Serena sat in Will's lap and they didn't stop talking until dawn.

They seemed to have an infinite number of things in common. Both of them had owned guinea pigs named Mabel as children, they'd each been dreadful at maths and, while both had failed their cycling proficiency test (the shame!), they were excellent pianists, both of them Grade 8. As well as discovering that Will's favourite ice cream was pistachio and his last girlfriend's name Cordelia (how she immediately hated that name), Serena found out that he was a theology student. He was also the only child of highly scientific parents, a subject of intense interest to him.

'That's unusual. Science and religion don't usually mix, do they?' she asked.

'True, though wasn't it Einstein who said that science without religion is lame, and religion without science is blind?'

'No idea!' laughed Serena. 'So you want to be a vicar?'

'I know it's not cool, not remotely, but yes.'

'Why?' she asked. 'Are your parents religious as well as scientific, just like Einstein?' she gently teased.

'No, not at all,' Will said, acknowledging Serena's teasing with a smile, and slightly shifting her weight on his lap. 'But we holidayed every summer in a place called Potter's Cove down in South Devon. We never ever went to church usually, but whenever we were there we always went to church on Sunday. The vicar there was a blast. Bernie Pemberton, he was called. Still is, I assume, though I haven't seen him in years. He was an old friend of my father and just the most captivating person. Full of fun, but compassionate too, and I could see that being a vicar was a vocation for him. It was his life. That's what I want. A job that actually makes a difference and that consumes you entirely. I'm resigned to being poor, but I've never been rich, and thankfully I've no desire for fast cars or flashy gadgets. It's a passion-killer though. Too many girls have run a mile when I've told them my plans. So if you're going to break my heart, beautiful Serena, do it now before it's too late.'

Serena giggled and knocked back another glass of acidic wine. 'I'll tell you what,' she said, 'I promise you now I won't break your heart, but I have two conditions. I don't want to get married, ever.'

Will raised his eyebrows. 'Okay,' he agreed. 'And the other?'

'I don't care how poor you are, we have to drink better wine than this.' They laughed and then they kissed. After that, they were inseparable.

The last evening of term, they'd lain squashed in Serena's single bed, legs entwined.

'Have you ever played the dinner party game?' Will asked.

'I don't think so. What is it?'

'You have to think of which famous people you'd invite to a dinner party if you could ask anyone – dead or alive.'

'Oooh, I love games like this. Let me think. I love the royals so I think I'd have to invite Princess Diana – she was so intriguing. And the princes. They're so cute and they'd get to see their mum again. They'd love that.'

'That's possibly putting a little more thought into the game than I'd expected,' Will said, amused. 'Who else?'

'Robbie Williams, for eye candy.'

'Repulsive-looking, if you ask me.'

'I'm not asking you,' Serena teased. 'Definitely Henry VIII, to try to work out why he was such a nutter. And Louis Theroux. You know – the journalist-broadcaster guy – to draw it all out of him. Have you seen *Weird Weekends*?' Will nodded. 'I love him,' Serena continued. 'My secret crush.'

'I'm beginning to wish I'd never started this game,' Will laughed.

'Well, I'm sure you'd want to invite some gorgeous ladies. Let me guess who you'd ask. Kylie, I bet. And I know you love Julia Roberts. Stephen Fry – I've seen his books on your shelf. Do you like Chris Evans? I bet you do!'

'I do, actually! They're pretty good guesses. But you're wrong. I wouldn't invite any of them.'

'Who would you ask then?'

'Just you.'

Serena looked at him and laughed tenderly. 'You old softie,' she teased, but then she became more serious. 'You're a keeper,' she told him.

'Do you mind . . . Can I ask . . . Serena, why don't you want to get married?'

Serena sighed and nestled herself into Will's arms. 'It's a long story. My first boyfriend, Freddie, promised me the world – including marriage. We didn't get engaged but he did buy me a ring. I was wildly in love. I imagined we'd stay together, get married, have kids. Then he met Luna. She wanted him and Luna always gets what she wants. She seduced him.'

'No way! Serena, that's horrendous.' Will looked appalled. 'He must have been a complete idiot!'

'Impulsive. Rash. That was half the trouble with Freddie.'

'What happened then? Did they go out with each other?'

'Oh, goodness, no! Freddie realised his mistake instantly and Luna didn't love him. She probably didn't even fancy him. She was just jealous and competitive and driven by some compulsion to steal him because he was mine. Anyway, that's why I don't want to get married. I know it's silly – it's not like I was jilted or anything. But I judge relationships by different standards these days. I don't need a ring or a bit of paper to represent commitment. Either we're committed or we're not.'

'Fair enough,' Will replied. 'And I don't blame you for feeling that way. If you ever change your mind though, you'd better let me know.'

'I won't. But thank you.' Serena kissed him and looked into his eyes. Will was a keeper alright.

He even came to stay with Serena and her family for a few days after Christmas and met Luna and the dreaded Colin. With Will there by her side, Serena found herself better able to suffer her sister and she was thrilled to see Will and her father getting on famously. They snuck off to the pub together and Will showed a genuine interest in the many books lining the shelves in Arthur's study.

Will saw the best in everyone, even Luna, and Serena found this wonderful character trait rubbing off on her. Suddenly, life had never seemed better.

These are the good old days, she thought, imagining herself looking back on them one day. She never wanted them to end.

17.
MAY 2015

May had arrived and Serena had developed an unexpected friendship with Alice, bonded by their experience the previous month. She'd begun to realise that underneath Alice's cool and prickly surface lay a genuinely lovely person. She was gradually becoming a true ally, or what Mrs Pipe would call a 'bread-and-cheese friend'.

There was a series of churchly events on the calendar and Alice was helping Serena arrange them, in her element as a former events organiser. There was the summer fete due to take place in June and plans already needed to be considered for the famous Harvest Supper, which, while months away in October, was apparently the highlight of the village calendar.

'Tell me about the Harvest Supper,' Serena asked Alice one day as they companionably untangled bunting to be used for the fete.

'Very smart affair, always has been,' replied Alice, attacking a particularly stubborn knot. 'Everyone in the village gets dolled up to the nines and the church hall is transformed. Caterers provide exquisite canapés and offer round champagne. There's a string quartet usually, or something similar. It's a bit of a highlight round here.'

'It sounds expensive to put on.'

'Oh, it's ticketed. Quite expensive, but everyone forks out for it. Think it makes everyone feel a little bit glamorous. Your eyes are as wide as saucers. You don't need to worry; I'll help you. But let's concentrate on one thing at a time. First, the fete.'

Later that day, Serena decided to call a house meeting. She wanted to try to get to the bottom of the uneasy feeling that had started to plague her since Mrs Pipe had told her about the dratted curse. On the whole, the house felt very warm and welcoming now, with the renovation almost complete. The walls were freshly painted, the master bedroom had a working fireplace and the rooms were becoming much homelier as second-hand furniture was unearthed by Serena, usually accompanied by either Ashna or Alice, at various markets and auctions in the area. Flowers, picked from the wild garden outside, were always present on various surfaces, and Serena had injected her own country cottage style throughout – ginghams, stripes and vintage floral prints.

But whenever she went into the nursery, Serena had this feeling. It was perhaps too flimsy to hold weight in convincing anyone else, but was too strong now to be ignored.

She'd tried to talk to Will about it on a couple of occasions, but the first time he'd quickly changed the topic of conversation and the second they'd been interrupted by Pete. She might have imagined it, but she thought she'd seen a look of relief on Will's face. In the end, she'd decided that if she couldn't get Will to discuss it on their own, she'd bring it up with everyone. They needed to chat about the upcoming fete anyway, so she would kill two birds with one stone.

'What's all this about then, my lovely?' asked Will as he handed gin and tonics to Serena, Ashna and Pete – concocted to perfection with two fingers of gin to five of tonic, masses of ice and a generous slice of lime.

'Delicious,' said Serena, taking a large gulp. 'Well, let's deal with the fete first,' she suggested. 'And then we'll get onto the other thing.'

'Good plan,' replied Will. 'Actually, house meetings are a great idea. They appeal to me; you know what I'm like,' he said, grinning. 'We should have them on a regular basis. Now, let's have a look at this list Alice has made. So we've booked a face-painter, a bouncy castle, nail-painting, pony rides, an acrobat – heavens, it's not that fellow who comes to church is it? The one with the suit and tie who says he used to work in a circus, but looks like he's never stepped foot outside an office in his life?'

'That's the one!' said Serena. 'Don't worry, Will. Ashna and I were treated to a taster before we booked him and he's amazing, honestly.'

'Mmm,' Will replied, remaining sceptical. 'If you say so. Right, so the stalls then. We're using the trestle tables from the hall and we've got a tombola, a raffle, home-knitted dolls, cakes, jewellery made by Alice (clever Alice, I didn't know she could make jewellery) and scarves and bedspreads made by our very own, incredibly talented Ashna . . .'

Ashna blushed. 'I hope some of the stuff sells . . . I've got masses of things now I've been working up in the attic. It's been fantastic, especially since Mrs Pipe found me that second-hand sewing machine.'

'She's a help, isn't she, in that dark and mysterious way of hers. Mrs Danvers from *Rebecca*, that's who she always reminds me of. Just a hint of something sinister about her.'

'Will, that's so mean,' said Serena. 'But very, very true!' she added, laughing nervously. 'Actually, perhaps now is a good time to tell you about the other thing. Now, please don't tell me I'm going mad, but I think Mrs Pipe might have been right. I think there may be a curse on the house. I get this feeling . . . It's the nursery . . .' she told them, tailing off as she saw their faces. Everyone looked at her, aghast. There was silence, followed by the clink of a piece of ice settling in Serena's glass.

Will raised his eyebrows. 'Well, somehow I wasn't expecting that,' he said at last. 'What on earth gives you that idea? I thought you'd dismissed that nonsense the day Mrs Pipe mentioned it,' he said. Although now he thought about it, he remembered how upset Serena had been and perhaps she had tried to mention it again on a couple of occasions since. Had he been burying his head in the sand about it all? He feared he probably had.

'A curse?' asked Pete, his dark blue eyes wide with intrigue and amusement. 'I knew there was a catch to this place. You've all been pretendin' to be friendly folk who'll forgive me my terrible past, but all along you were lurin' me into your House of Horrors. You're never gonna let me go, are you?' he stage-whispered.

'Sssh,' said Ashna. 'It's not funny, Pete.' Ashna could be blunt with Pete; their relationship had become cosy and comfortable. Serena still had high hopes of getting them together, but for now she leapt at Ashna's apparent solidarity.

'Have you felt it too?' asked Serena, full of hope.

'Well, no, but it's been a busy time for you moving into a new place, a new parish, with the renovation to sort out and the village events to organise. Perhaps you're a little stressed? Maybe that's the trouble? I could help you. Teach you some yoga or meditation?' she offered sweetly.

And there it was. Will was the sceptic she had known he would be. Pete thought it was highly funny. And even Ashna, sweet Ashna, thought it was all in her mind. The meeting had been a bad idea. If she was going to get to the bottom of this curse, it was clear she was going to have to do it alone.

18.
DECEMBER 2001

Having graduated in the summer, Serena and Will were living together in Will's parish in Hither Green in South East London, where he'd started his first job as a curate (an assistant vicar) for St Swithuns. He was having to endure being treated with some disdain by the parish vicar – the Reverend Pankhurst.

Since Serena had moved in with him to the tiny terraced house that came with his post, she'd realised that living with a vicar was a job in itself. But she embraced it wholeheartedly, being as committed to life as the partner of a curate as she was to Will himself.

The couple enjoyed a straightforward relationship from the start. No games. No indecision. They loved each other. They were nice to each other. It was all very simple. There was just one blight on this perfect landscape. One bone of contention. Serena wanted a baby. And Will didn't. Or at least, not yet.

'Serena, you're an enigma to me about this. All your friends are raring to start careers. We're so young. Only twenty-one. We have no money. You don't even want to get married. Why a baby?'

But Serena couldn't explain it. It was an urge. An overwhelming urge. Perhaps if she'd followed her original dream to train as a midwife, she'd have been in less of a hurry, but she hadn't, and the thought of more exams at this stage made her feel sick. She didn't care that Will was only a curate with a wage that was laughable. She wanted a career, of course she did, after achieving a First in her languages degree. But there was plenty of time for all that. The priority for her was to have children. She adored Will and she wanted half a dozen little Wills. They would fit into their lives and follow her around like ducklings. She was a natural nurturer and had all the impatience of a twenty-something who felt as though life – real, grown-up life – should start right now.

Will was adamant, however, and she knew she'd already pushed him enough on the subject. She put her desires to one side for now and found herself a job as a translator for an international logistics company. It wasn't her dream job (she'd far rather have been starting work as a midwife), but it would do and the salary was decent.

Christmas was upon them and they were heading to Sussex to spend a week with the Meadows family. Predictably, Colin was now history, but Luna had another new boyfriend and, while Will was excited about meeting this Sebastian, Serena was simply bracing herself.

But Christmas turned out to be magical from the moment they arrived until the time they left. Sebastian was surprisingly charming – not in a slimy way, but in an easy-going, comfortable and happy-to-join-in-with-chores kind of way. Luna was relaxed and far less moody than usual, perhaps finally in love.

On Christmas Eve, the whole family put up a huge tree in the sitting room and Serena found an old Christmas CD, so they all danced about to the usual festive favourites while they decorated the branches. They argued playfully over the winner of the best Christmas song of all time, about which they all had strong opinions (Nat King Cole's 'The Christmas Song', as far as Serena was concerned).

Then, while Stephanie clattered about in the kitchen making supper, everyone else pottered across to the Rose and Crown for a few drinks and Serena and Luna found themselves bumping into old friends they hadn't seen in years. Eventually they returned home for a delicious, warming casserole and Serena gave her mother a hug, recognising she'd gone to a lot of effort as cooking wasn't usually her forte.

On Christmas Day, Serena, Sebastian and Arthur busied themselves making the lunch together while Will drove back to London first thing to assist the vicar with the morning's service at his parish church (the poor fellow had only driven back and forth to London the night before to help with Midnight Mass). He made it back just as lunch was served and everyone was merrily pulling crackers and exclaiming over the tacky gifts within. Stephanie and Luna had spent the morning glamming themselves up and both looked stunning, while Serena still had her apron on and her make-up-free face was, she was sure, unbecomingly shiny. But she didn't care. They were all together and everyone was in high spirits.

On Christmas night, after a raucous game of charades, Arthur announced himself in need of some peace and quiet and sloped off to his study while everyone else flicked through the channels deciding which festive special to enjoy. The chosen programme didn't appeal to Serena so she helped herself to a glass of champagne and pottered along to find her father.

Serena saw Arthur a moment before he caught sight of her and she was taken aback for, seeing him there in his armchair, enjoying a brandy, she realised he had somehow – and quite without her realising it – grown old. She felt a momentary shiver of sadness pass through her. Then he spotted her, looked up and smiled – immediately seeming much younger.

'Mind if I join you?' Serena asked.

'I'd love you to. Your favourite beanbag is still available. I can't believe it's lasted all these years. Never had the heart to throw it out, although it seems a bit weedy. I'm sure it's lost most of its filling.'

Serena plonked herself down opposite her father and they beamed at each other contentedly, knowing they would either chat or not bother and either way, it wouldn't matter.

'Luna seems happy,' Arthur remarked at last, cradling his drink and resting it on the paunch of his stomach.

'I know, on really good form. Seb seems to have made all the difference. I hope it lasts. What do you think of him?'

'A solid chap, much better than any of the previous ones. Do you remember Colin last year? Sat there through Christmas lunch eating with his mouth open. I couldn't sit opposite him any longer – had to switch places with you!'

Serena snorted with laughter. 'Don't!' she said. 'I couldn't work out what you were playing at and then I looked across the table and realised why you'd wanted to swap. It was so gross!'

'He didn't get any of our jokes either . . . I shouldn't be mean, but he was a complete dullard. I don't know what Luna saw in him.'

'Nor do I, but thankfully he's history. Seb seems much more hopeful. Good table manners, happy to help and – most of all – capable of improving Luna's mood. I don't think we could ask for more!'

'I know she's difficult,' Arthur said. 'But, you know, when I was growing up as a Barnardo's child, in and out of children's homes, my one wish was that I had a sibling – someone with whom I could have an unspoken understanding. Every night I used to dream about having a brother. When I met Clive all those years later, it really was a dream coming true. I know it's a bit different as he and I are so similar. But blood's thicker than water, my darling. Always remember that.'

'I know,' Serena replied. She'd never told her father about the incident with Freddie, but he knew more than anyone what a test it had been to be a sister to Luna. 'And I really think she's changing. Seb's going to be the making of her.'

'She'll marry this one,' Arthur said. 'You mark my words.'

'Maybe,' agreed Serena. 'You'll never have to give me away though, Dad. Never getting married,' she declared and she jumped up and gave her dad a hug.

⁊◠⁊

Despite Seb's good influence, Serena still kept expecting Luna's mood to darken as the days passed, but when they reached the day of their departure, she was relieved to find there had been no incidents nor even any sour-looking faces during the whole festive period.

They arrived home the day before New Year's Eve and Will decided to pick up takeaway fish and chips from the chippy around the corner as there was no food in the house.

'Won't be long. Warm the plates,' he said, planting a kiss on Serena's lips, then whistling as he zipped himself into his jacket and slammed the door behind him.

Serena had just unpacked when she heard her phone ringing.

'Hel-lo,' she sang out, having located her mobile.

'Serena, it's your mother,' Stephanie started quietly. 'It's bad news, I'm afraid . . . Your father. I don't know how to say this, Serena. It's just so dreadful. Serena, he's died. He's dead.' Her voice was louder now. 'He's had a heart attack. He's dead. Dead!' she almost screamed, sobbing down the phone, and Serena noticed, in a strangely detached kind of way, that this was the first time she'd ever heard her mother cry.

'I'll call you back,' Serena had whispered and crawled into bed where she lay, unmoving, until Will returned with the fish and chips.

Serena began her grieving feeling like a ship that had capsized and was left bobbing around in the ocean. Banjaxed. That was the only word to describe it. She couldn't cry for the first week and then, when she did, she barely stopped. She was a soggy mess. Then she was angry. Then, as the weeks passed, Serena became just quietly sad. Will wondered if she was depressed, but Serena knew it was grief and that there was a long road ahead of her. She thought about what her friend Lisa had said, who'd lost her mother as a teenager: '*There's no place to hide from grief. You can't climb over it or slide under it. You just have to go through it.*'

Will found it hard to see Serena like this. He liked solutions and there simply didn't seem to be a way to fix this. Until, finally, he had an idea.

'Serena, my lovely,' he said, finding her lying quietly in the bath one evening.

'Mmm,' she replied, looking up at him with a faint smile.

'I've changed my mind,' he told her. 'Let's try for a baby.'

PART TWO

19.
JUNE 2015

Serena had always enjoyed the elements. She loved nothing more than pulling on an anorak and pacing through fields or running along a beach in the pouring rain, enjoying the wild exhilaration given freely by Mother Nature.

But even she had to admit that such weather was not ideal for a summer fete. Will and Alice had been incredibly organised about the preparations and every possible detail had been considered. But they couldn't organise the weather.

Serena arrived at Alice's house, a huge Georgian pile a short stroll away from the Vicarage. She'd never been inside but Alice had invited her for coffee before they made their way to the playing fields to set up for the fete. As expected, the interior of the house was immaculate. White walls (no scuffs), white sofas (no stains), white tiled floors (no marks). It was pristine, the only colour provided by vast and modern pieces of artwork dominating the walls. As Serena walked along the hallway into the state-of-the-art kitchen, following Alice's upright back and shiny hair, she wondered if Alice was a natural perfectionist or whether, for some reason, she'd developed into one. Either way, it seemed to Serena that Alice held a tension about her, always present in her jaw, that couldn't be healthy. Still, it wasn't for Serena to tell her this and she now knew that, underneath the brittle exterior, Alice was actually a very kind-hearted person. She'd been an absolute brick about the fete.

'I simply can't believe this weather,' said Alice, switching on the coffee machine, which made all sorts of impressive-sounding splutters. 'The forecast said it was going to be fair,' she added, clearly most put out that the weather wasn't playing ball.

'I know, it's so typical, isn't it?' replied Serena, peering out of the windows as she accepted a tiny cup of espresso. The rain showed no sign of abating. 'But the show must go on. We'll just have to put up some canopies to protect the goods on show. We'd better tell the acrobat to be careful too. We could do without being sued!' she laughed. 'Will's going to meet us there, by the way. He's just finishing off a wedding interview with Fay Holland.'

'Ah, yes, the gypsy family of Cattlebridge. He'd better make it a good service or old Mrs Holland will cast a spell on him! Every house in the village is brimming with dried lavender, as we all know she'll curse us if we refuse to buy a bunch when we walk past her on the high street. So silly, but you never want to test these things, do you?'

'No, you don't,' answered Serena, reminded of the supposed curse on the Vicarage. She considered confiding in Alice about it all, but she couldn't bear the thought of another friend thinking she was losing the plot so she drained her espresso without mentioning it.

'Shall we get going?' she asked and, after attiring themselves in suitable raincoats, they traipsed out into the deluge.

⚬⚬

The fete was a disaster. There was no other way to describe it. The turnout was dreadfully poor, with few villagers tempted to splash around a sodden field when they could be warm and dry at home or at least undercover in a shopping centre. Then there was an incident with a catering van serving undercooked chicken and sparking a salmonella scare (nobody would know until a little later whether this was justified – a nerve-racking wait for anyone who'd sampled a chicken burger).

To add to the calamity, the pony rides had to be cancelled, as the lady who owned the ponies didn't want her prized possessions catching a cold, and the face-painter failed to turn up, meaning a small gaggle of young girls left the fete disappointed. Even the acrobat, the much publicised highlight, was a damp squib, turning up with his arm in a sling after showing off some of his tricks in the pub the previous evening. Will was unusually despondent and when the man attempted to walk the tightrope regardless and fell heavily to the ground (hurting, it seemed, his good arm) it was he who, resigned, drove the acrobat to the local Accident and Emergency Department.

Serena had decided it simply couldn't get any worse when she heard Ashna shouting.

'Get off me!' she was yelling. 'Get away! I hate you both! How did you even find me?'

Serena saw two men trying to grab Ashna as she fought them off with all her might, tipping her stall to the ground and covering the sodden grass with all her beautiful scarves and bedspreads. The men had to be her father and brother. How on earth had they found her? Serena, panicking, ran over and tried her best to extricate Ashna from the men, but she was no match for them and was shoved into the bushes for her trouble. By now, a crowd had gathered and a frisson of excitement was evident at this unexpectedly dramatic turn of events. The villagers watched avidly but not one of them stepped in to assist. Serena was desperately looking around for backup when she spotted Max and Pete storming across the field, barging the crowd out of the way and coming to Ashna's rescue.

'Oh, thank goodness,' Serena muttered to herself, but this was just the beginning. Max and Pete managed to pull Ashna's father and brother away for long enough for her to escape and she ran towards Serena, sobbing. Serena was just calming her friend down, planning to escort her away as soon as possible, when she saw that matters had turned violent.

Ashna's brother, a giant of a man, had walloped Pete, who was now lying on the ground, winded. It wasn't long before he was back up on his feet though, and he retaliated like the ex-convict he was, landing several punches. They were decent whacks, but Ashna's brother proved resilient.

Max had been employing a more peaceful approach, simply trying to restrain Ashna's father while shouting at the crowd to call the police, but all of a sudden he fell victim to the brother's effective right hook. He was sent reeling and landed with a thud. And as he reached up to his bloody nose, a strange thing happened. He started to cry and shake, bawling like a baby. This seemed to take every-one by surprise – even Ashna's brother. The crowd stared, open-mouthed, as Max continued to whimper.

Fortunately, at this moment the police arrived and soon Ashna's father and brother were carted off in a van while a kindly police-woman took Ashna back to the dry warmth of the Vicarage so she could give a statement. The crowd began to disperse, with only a few glances still being cast in the direction of the weeping Max, and Serena – having dispatched Ashna and the policewoman – went to his side. Pete was there, ineffectually rubbing Max's shoulders.

'It's okay,' Serena said to Pete. 'You head home and get the kettle on. I'll help Max.' Pete disappeared with a look of relief on his face. 'Look at me, Max,' said Serena calmly, and he did as he was told. She inspected his face. His nose was a little bloody, but not so bad, cer-tainly nothing to warrant such an extreme emotional reaction. 'You're fine, Max,' she told him, pressing a tissue to his nose. 'Now take some deep breaths and then we're going to walk back to the Vicarage, okay? Can you manage to walk?'

Max nodded, starting to calm himself at last. He hobbled along with Serena, a shadow of his usually hearty self.

∽

Back at the Vicarage, Ashna and the policewoman were in the study and Pete, having boiled the kettle as requested, had taken himself upstairs for a shower to warm up and clean his own bloody nose.

Max sat down at the kitchen table, head in hands, while Serena made them both hot chocolate. She pushed a mug towards him, sitting down opposite at the pine table.

'Max?' asked Serena gently. Max had been looking anywhere but at her until now, but he bravely lifted his gaze to hers.

He said, 'I feel such a fool. Such an idiot. You're thinking I'm a total wimp, right?'

'I'm thinking there's more to this than meets the eye,' replied Serena.

Max sighed. 'Do you remember when you first met me? I arrived at the house without my overalls on and you couldn't believe somebody so posh would be a painter and decorator?'

Serena nodded, still embarrassed.

'Well, the truth is, I wasn't always a painter and decorator. My father was a lawyer, my mother a GP. I've got several siblings – my older brother became an architect, one of my sisters followed Dad's footsteps and became a lawyer and the other is a professional dancer. I'm the youngest and I always wanted to be a doctor like Mum. So I trained for years and specialised in general practice. I became a GP and was really happy in my job. Then I met Lara.

My wife,' he explained, and Serena raised her eyebrows, wondering where all this was going.

'You're married?' she asked. For some reason she'd thought of Max as an eternal bachelor, cheerfully sporting the checked shirts he favoured (and clearly, by their appearance, struggled to iron himself), with just his lovely dogs for company.

'Sadly, yes,' he said, and his eyes again filled with tears.

'Are you still together? What happened?' asked Serena, imagining that perhaps she'd suffered some terrible tragedy and died or perhaps they'd endured a painful break-up.

'She's lucky she's not in prison.'

'Prison?' she repeated, shocked. 'Good heavens, what on earth did she do?'

Max scrunched up his eyes. 'She tormented me, bullied me, pushed me down the stairs, hit me, slammed my fingers in the door, made me doubt myself until I had to give up my job, my friends, everything. Shit, I haven't told anyone about this since I made a fresh start here in the village. Today, being punched, it just brought it all back. I hadn't realised how much I'm still affected by everything that happened.' Max paused.

'You know the worst thing of all?' he asked. 'Nobody believed me. Even after the final incident, before I moved away, there was so much doubt. Even my family and friends doubted me. I mean, I'm not small and pathetic-looking, am I? No one could understand how I wasn't able to stand up for myself. Especially as Lara's about five foot tall and the most charming woman you're likely to come across. But she was so clever. She eroded my confidence – and I'm usually a confident guy, as you've probably gathered by now. She did it so cleverly. Until, actually, I felt I deserved everything I got.'

Serena was desperately sad for Max. How horrendous to have endured what he'd been through and then have everybody doubt him.

'What was the final incident?' she asked.

'She tried to poison my dogs,' Max said, crumpling, and Serena pushed back her chair and wrapped Max in a firm hug as he sobbed and sobbed into her long blonde hair.

20.
SUMMER 2002

Serena was feeling much, much better. Her grief for her father, while still ready to pounce at inopportune moments, was largely under control. The turning point for Serena had been finding an old poetry book of her father's, in which she'd found a scrap of paper written in his unmistakable calligraphy. She'd been home to visit her mother and while Stephanie endeavoured to produce some supper, Serena had ventured into Arthur's study, finding it untouched and lifeless. She'd almost walked straight back out again, but a strong impulse had drawn her towards his books, in particular a tome by the name of *Other Men's Flowers*. It was tucked within this that she'd found the scrap of paper. It was headed with the simple title 'Butterfly'. Serena sat down in her father's armchair to read it:

One day, I won't be sitting in this chair.
I'm getting older, my heart and soul are shadows now
compared to those days before. It makes me think, from time to
time, about what happens next. Will I sleep forever, like an
anaesthetised body never coming round, or will there be
something else? People talk about heaven, and seeing long-missed
relatives again, but such a prospect irks me. I don't

want to see the mother who deserted me, nor the man who failed to bring me up. No. For me, heaven would be to be alone, floating where I wish. A butterfly. A Red Admiral. For me, that would be bliss.

Serena had found her eyes filling with tears at the bittersweet poignancy of her father's poem, but it was a gift as well. Since then, whenever she saw the distinctive Red Admiral, she smiled and greeted it: 'Hello, Dad.' It was the most enormous comfort.

Soon after Will's suggestion in February, they'd started to try for a baby as well, and there was nothing like the promise of new life to assist in moving on. Nothing had happened instantly, but it didn't bother her unduly. For one thing, they were distracted by their busy lives – Serena's job as a translator, Will's parish in Hither Green, their friends and hectic social life.

Meanwhile, her relationship with Luna seemed to be improving, in part as a result of their shared grief in the aftermath of Arthur's death and also down to the fact that, having settled into a steady relationship with Seb, Luna was currently in very high spirits.

It was a Friday night and Will and Serena were meeting Luna and Sebastian for dinner. They were dining at Luna's favourite eatery, Veeraswamy – an upmarket Indian restaurant on Regent Street.

'Amazing to see you both,' Luna gushed. Her eyes glittered and, as they all sat down and began ordering drinks, Serena caught sight of something else that was sparkling. She squealed.

'Luna! That ring!'

Luna smiled a wide smile – the cat who'd got the cream. Will observed her with interest. She and Serena were still identical, but distinctive nonetheless. It wasn't just that Luna's lashes were long and spidery, enhanced by sooty mascara, while Serena's were flatter and shorter. Nor was it that Luna's lips were juicy and red, where Serena's were pale and a little chapped. They were both beautiful

– one natural, one oozing glamour – but to Will, it was their characters that, even when you caught a mere glimpse of them, really set them apart. Serena, always gentle, and her twin perpetually glittering, whether with fun or rage or danger.

Luna proffered her hand towards Serena, grinning proudly, and Seb wrapped an arm around her shoulder.

'Call me a glutton for punishment,' he smiled. 'But I asked Luna last night if she'd do me the honour of being my wife and, as you can see, she said yes!'

'Oh, that's wonderful news,' said Serena, reaching across to hug Luna, then Seb, while Will called the waiter back and asked to replace their drinks order with a bottle of chilled champagne.

'Tell me all about it,' Serena said, once all four glasses had been poured. And she sat back and listened happily to Luna's evident excitement. This, thought Serena, could be the very making of her sister. Serena didn't want to get married herself, but for Luna it had come to mean the world: total acceptance into the life of another person. Perhaps she'd always felt lacking, with a twin so different from her. Always seeking to fill a void.

Serena thought back to their childhood and, despite how difficult Luna had been, found herself feeling sorry for the moody child she remembered, who'd found Serena so disappointingly dissimilar to herself. Even as newborns Luna had been the more dominant (arriving first and weighing in two pounds heavier than her sister), but for all her supremacy, Serena suspected that what she'd always craved was for her twin to be more like her: to be someone she could gossip with, and with whom she could discuss friends and hairstyles and clothes and make-up. Someone she could be one with.

Perhaps the competitive side of Luna had developed after realising that close kinship she'd been promised in the womb would never come to fruition as they grew up. If she couldn't be united with Serena, then she would be better than her. This neediness in Luna, coupled with her relentless competitiveness, had been exhausting for Serena. As she took another sip of champagne, she realised she was thrilled that Luna had fallen for Seb and found someone she could be soulmates with – not just because it meant her twin was happy at last, but also because it felt as though, for her, the pressure was off.

Serena caught Luna and Seb exchange a glance and there was a moment of tenderness between them. Yes, thought Serena. There was no doubt about it. Luna had found her perfect match and, as a result, it seemed she was definitely changing. For the better.

21.
JULY 2015

The start of the summer had been predictably changeable, but at last it seemed to have begun in earnest, not that this did much to lighten the general mood at the Vicarage. It seemed the fete had signalled the start of trouble for all the occupants of the house. Ashna had taken on a hunted look, her large eyes constantly watchful, even though her father and brother had been bailed on the strict condition of not going within five hundred yards of her. As well as being investigated for the assault on Max and causing an affray, they were suspected of new offences relating to forced marriage under the Anti-social Behaviour, Crime and Policing Act 2014. But Ashna was nervous – they knew where she was now, after all – and had retreated into herself.

Max was equally subdued and no longer sang as he worked around the house. Even Pete seemed a little quieter. And for Will and Serena, it felt as if there had been a seismic shift in the village. When they'd first moved to Cattlebridge, they'd expected to be received with hesitation: of course a new vicar had to work hard to win round the villagers. But it was as though, having started to engender support, the tide had suddenly started to turn against them. The disastrous fete hadn't helped, but events the previous weekend seemed to have cemented the start of bad feeling.

In an attempt to throw himself into village life, Will had decided to take part in a local cricket match on the Saturday. The morning had gone well and he'd just got his fifty when he spotted Serena running across the pitch looking panic-stricken.

'Will, the wedding! You're late for Fay Holland's wedding. Had you forgotten? It was meant to start at midday. The bride's there already!'

Will paled immediately and ditched his bat, making hurried excuses and legging it to the church in his cricket whites. He arrived, panting, and – after apologising profusely to the bride, who was waiting in the churchyard, chewing gum laboriously, her eyes vacant and her expression grim – he scurried into the vestry where he slipped his cassock on over his whites, pads and all.

After that, Will put on a sterling performance and the service went without a hitch, but he was not going to be let off the hook by the Holland family, old gypsy stock and the least forgiving sorts to live in the village. Old Mrs Holland gave him a cold, hard stare as she left the church. She said nothing, but there was a challenge in the way she looked at him. Will felt a sense of dread creep over him.

During the week that followed, a further incident had occurred that had also blotted Will's copybook. Another influential family in the village were the Huntingdon-Loxleys: an incredibly important family in the village. Or at least, they thought they were. Granny Huntingdon-Loxley, the matriarch, had finally given in to the inevitability of death at the grand age of ninety-seven and her funeral had taken place on Tuesday. The memorial service itself had been just right, but Granny Huntingdon-Loxley had chosen to be cremated, which necessitated a further service at the crematorium in Hastings later the same day. Pete needed to head into town, so after the memorial he cadged a lift. He offered to drive, as Will always found it a little constricting to drive in his cassock. The traffic was heavy, which wasn't a good start, but eventually they arrived. Will spotted the mourners gathered in a huddle by the crematorium.

'Won't be long,' Will said to Pete. 'About half an hour, so you take the car and then meet me back here when you've finished in town.'

'Okey dokey,' said Pete. 'I only need to pop into one shop. Might just have a quick fag here, before I go.' He got out, and drifted off to a patch of grass far away from the milling crowd. Will walked towards the group, who looked sombre and forbidding and then, as Will approached, somewhat alarmed. He immediately checked his flies. *What's the problem?* he wondered and then froze as his car slowly crept past him down the hill towards the crematorium.

'Aaargh!' he cried and ran ahead, desperately trying to open the driver's door as the car inched forward – he usually kept his car unlocked now they lived in the countryside, but Pete (knowing what criminals could be like) had locked it. 'Pete!' Will bellowed back towards his friend and Pete, who'd been obliviously smoking his cigarette, looked up in horror. He raced down the hill towards Will and the crawling car, but he was too late. The car crashed loudly and definitely into the wall, exposing the cremation chamber.

Will had apologised to the horrified family and, once practicalities had been dealt with, he had proceeded (in some fluster) to conduct the cremation. But the Huntingdon-Loxleys were unimpressed and he suspected that – like the Hollands – they held some sway in the village.

ᕦᕤ

When Will saw how thin his ordinarily decent-sized congregation was at church today, he realised just how grave his two mistakes had been. His fears were confirmed in the pub after church as well, when a number of usually friendly villagers snubbed him as he tried to engage them in chatter while he enjoyed his post-service pint.

At lunch, the glum occupants of the Vicarage congregated for a roast in the kitchen and discussed what they could possibly do to restore the villagers' faith in Will and Serena.

'How about a youth club?' suggested Max, who, while not exactly a resident at the Vicarage, had become a part of the family (along with his dogs), joining in with meals most days – particularly Will's famous Sunday roasts.

'That's not a bad idea,' replied Will, pushing back his hair. 'The kids are always hanging around in the park or outside the shops, with nothing to do. The hard thing will be trying to get them interested. I remember being fifteen: you'd have had to entice me with serious amounts of money to get me to join any club.'

'Yeah, me too,' agreed Pete. 'You know what they did at the prison though, to get the inmates to join stuff?'

Everyone looked at him, intrigued. Pete was always full of interesting stories about his time inside.

'Food,' he announced. 'Crisps, doughnuts, nothing too healthy. That'll draw 'em in. And a bit of competition too. You should've seen us all one time when the wardens started a tiddlywinks competition. All these grown men desperate to win – and the cheers from my mates when I was the champion . . . It was brilliant.'

Will smiled and took a gulp of wine. 'You know what? That's an excellent idea. Let's do it. We can set it up in the church hall – maybe on a Friday evening. But I'm fairly sure the fact I'm a vicar will put them off if I try to run it. I think I need to find someone a bit younger and less . . . well, vicarly . . .'

'I'll do it,' said Ashna. She'd been quietly listening, but her voice now was clear and sincere. 'Actually, it will be good for me. Give me something to focus on. Would you trust me to run it?'

'Of course,' enthused Will. 'Ashna, that's so kind of you. You'll be perfect for the job.' He jumped up from his chair and gave her a big hug.

'Give me one of those too,' grinned Max, a glimmer of his usual cheerful character apparent again. 'I'll help Ashna. Keep all those rowdy boys in check. Even a wimp like me should be able to deal with a few cheeky youths,' he added, laughing at himself.

'Seriously?' asked Will.

'Seriously.'

Will gave Max a manly kind of hug, involving lots of backslapping, and Serena smiled at them as she started to clear the plates.

She was relieved they'd come up with a possible solution for getting the village back on side, but she was a little worried about the Harvest Supper, which they needed to think about too.

'What about the Harvest Supper?' she said, voicing her thoughts. 'What if we spend masses of money putting on this posh do and then nobody buys any tickets? If things carry on the way they are, everyone will boycott the event.'

'Has it been popular in the past?' asked Max.

'Yes, hugely. Very smart. Champagne, string quartet, the works.'

'Sounds boring to me,' Max replied. 'You know what I'd do if I were you? Change it up. It's a risk, of course, but it would solve the budget issue if you just did something much simpler and more rustic. You could hang hops up all over the hall and provide proper meals instead of those fiddly things that leave you starving. Then you wouldn't need to make it a ticketed event either – much more likely to get people coming along if you're not charging a fortune. Maybe you could just do a whip-round at the end to cover the costs or something?'

'That's an amazing idea,' agreed Will. 'We could bash out a load of tunes on the piano too, couldn't we, Serena? Some good old stirring hymns?'

'Perfect,' she smiled. The ideas were fantastic – she just hoped the risk would pay off.

They all felt a little more positive by the end of lunch, but Serena had to admit the mood of the house was affecting them not just as individuals, but she and Will as a couple as well, particularly since she'd decided to deal with her anxieties about the curse alone and couldn't confide in Will about them. It made her feel lonely, surrounded though she was by other people, including her partner.

Tomorrow, she decided, she would start her research. Somebody in the village must know about this wretched curse.

'*Knowledge is power*', she remembered Miss Jones saying once at primary school. If she could just find out a bit more about it, she was sure she'd begin to feel better.

22.
SUMMER 2003

It was the summer and Will and Serena were still living in Hither Green, where life was increasingly busy. In many ways, they were still in the honeymoon period of their relationship, but it wasn't without its tests. Serena loved helping parishioners and was totally on board with the many parish events she helped with, but she was starting to resent the fact that she and Will barely seemed to have a moment to themselves. Hardly an evening went by when they weren't disturbed at the dinner table by the vicar or his frighteningly bossy wife, ordering Will to take on yet more jobs – always of the least appealing variety, such as fundraising for the church roof, taking the early morning services and recruiting for the choir; not to mention liaising with the French organist Jean-Paul, who was an absolute pit bull.

The stress was heightened by the absence of any pregnancy. Over a period of eighteen months, they experienced increasing frustration, each month involving an exciting two-week wait followed by crushing disappointment. A fortnight before Luna and Seb's wedding, they finally reached the day of their appointment with a fertility expert.

'I see from your GP's letter that you've been trying for almost eighteen months now,' said the consultant, Mr Charterham, a small, precise-looking man who sat neatly in his large chair, his hands together, fingertips touching. His office on this humid July day was hot and stuffy, the only air an occasional warm waft from his desk fan.

'You're both very young, so that's a huge advantage, and it's not unusual for these things to take at least a year to eighteen months,' he continued. 'It's not necessarily an indicator of any problem. Is there a reason you wanted to see me at this relatively early stage?'

'Impatience, I guess,' explained Will. 'I suppose we both thought that – given we're so young – it would happen immediately. After about six months or so, we began to wonder if something might be wrong and we just thought it might be better to find that out sooner rather than later.'

'Very practical, and we can, of course, run various tests for you, but can I try you with my expert, non-medical advice first?' the consultant asked.

'Go ahead,' said Will, and Serena nodded in agreement, twirling a blonde curl around her finger.

'As soon as you start with investigations, you're going to be feeding your brain with the idea that there *is* a problem. The brain is probably the most important aspect when it comes to fertility. My advice would be to go away, keep trying, don't think about it too much. Relax. See what happens. You have time on your side. What do you think?'

'I think that makes perfect sense,' replied Will, with an audible sigh of relief. He hadn't been looking forward to providing a sample. But Serena cleared her throat.

'I do get what you're saying,' she said hesitantly. Serena was a natural people-pleaser, but not a pushover when it came to aspects of her life she considered of utmost importance. 'But I just have this feeling, like I know there's something wrong. For the sake of a few simple tests, I'd rather find out, if that's okay?' she asked, looking from Will to the consultant.

'Of course,' they both said, although they exchanged a small glance. Serena knew it was good advice, but she'd always had strong instincts, and she knew in her heart a proactive approach would be better. Now they'd actually managed to see the consultant, she couldn't bear to go away without taking some steps forward.

'Blood tests for you first,' Mr Charterham said, scribbling illegibly on a pad and passing the sheet of paper to Serena. 'You can get these taken on the ground floor of the hospital today. Once we have the results we can go from there. And for you, Mr Blacksmith, a sample pot . . . There's a room just next door. There are plenty of magazines to look at: *Steam Engines Monthly* and such like,' he said wryly. 'Please return the pot to my secretary. There's no rush,' he added, with a sympathetic smile. Will's face turned the colour of his hair. This was not the route he wanted to take at all, but as he watched Serena head off along the corridor towards the lift he saw a spring in her step. She was so desperately eager for this to happen. And if this was what it took to get them the baby she so badly wanted, then it was what he would do. He sighed and made his way into a small room and its selection of grubby, well-thumbed magazines.

༄

The day before Luna and Seb's wedding, they received the results.

'Mr Charterham here,' explained the voice at the other end of the telephone. Serena felt her heart rate accelerate as she realised this was it: the moment of truth.

'You have the results?' she asked. She jammed the handset between her ear and shoulder and searched around for a pen and pad. Will was helping the vicar shift some furniture around in the church and Serena had been scrubbing the bath when the telephone had rung. She'd scurried down the stairs to answer the phone, where it trilled into the narrow hallway.

'I do. Let me run you through them. First of all, I'm pleased to tell you your husband's results have come back clear. Nothing wrong with the motility or mobility there. And I can see from your blood test results that you have an abundance of eggs, which is also excellent. The rest of the results are within normal ranges too . . . There's just one that indicates a possible problem.'

Serena's heart sank. She stopped scribbling. She'd expected a problem – she'd felt it instinctively – but still, to have it confirmed . . . She took a deep breath.

'Yes?'

'It's the antinuclear antibody test we took . . . It's come back positive. I think you may be suffering with an autoimmune disorder. We'll run more tests but it looks like coeliac disease in your case. I'm surprised you haven't been suffering with any symptoms.'

'But what does that mean?' asked Serena.

'Well, an autoimmune disorder occurs when the immune system becomes confused and generates antibodies that attack the cells of the body even though they're not foreign invaders – in coeliac disease, the cells of the small intestine. The immune system is designed to detect and destroy foreign substances that enter the body, so a positive result like this sometimes crops up when women are struggling to get pregnant or suffering with frequent miscarriages . . . Look, I know this is a lot to take in,' Mr Charterham went on, 'but the good news is, there are medications you can take that usually manage this sort of thing, as well as approaching the problem from a nutritional angle. A gluten-free diet is a must. And . . . well, if these don't work, there are always other options . . .'

'Such as?' Serena asked.

'IVF, that sort of thing . . . But for now, let's take it one step at a time. I must say, I'm glad you didn't take my advice when I saw you. Much better to avoid multiple miscarriages, which I'm sorry to say would almost certainly have happened if we hadn't tested now. With autoimmune disorders, the body sees a foetus as a potentially dangerous infection in need of removal and develops antibodies to the baby.'

'That's something, I suppose. So what do we do now?'

'I'll get my secretary to call you next week to make a further appointment. We'll take some more tests and get you started on a course of medication. I'll refer you to a nutritionist as well. My dear, one way or another, we will do our best to get you a baby.'

Serena was crushed, but smiled wanly at the consultant's words. Avuncular was the word for him, she thought, but the call had certainly taken the wind out of her sails. Later, she explained it all to Will.

'*That* explains why you always feel grotty when you've eaten pasta! And I've always thought it's weird you don't like bread. Well, thank goodness we found out now,' he said, concentrating on the parts of the conversation that seemed the least upsetting.

'Exactly what the consultant said. And we're going to see him again very soon and get everything sorted, but for now can we just forget all about it and have fun at Luna's wedding tomorrow? Let's get really drunk and dance till the small hours.'

'Definitely,' said Will, relieved Serena was keen not to dwell on the diagnosis for the moment. Relieved too that they could stop worrying for a little while and enjoy their youth, as they should be doing right now. He couldn't wait for the party.

⁓

The following day dawned bright and cloudless. Serena and Will, feeling a weight lifted off their shoulders at finally having a diagnosis and a plan, arrived at the church in a state of high excitement. They were ushered to the correct pew, just behind Stephanie, who they kissed – which proved a little tricky as she was wearing an enormous statement hat with feathers on it that trembled when she moved. Serena's mother was sitting next to her friend, Sheila, and they continued their gossiping while Serena and Will both waved to the groom, who was standing at the front of the church looking suitably nervous.

'Poor Seb,' Serena whispered to Will. 'He looks like a rabbit in the headlights. You're lucky I'm never going to put you through this.'

Will was giggly, as he always was when he wasn't conducting or assisting with a service, and his mirth became contagious when he suddenly let rip an enormous fart. It was so loud they heard the Scottish woman sitting behind them chastise her husband.

'Angus! That's disgraceful. And in church too!'

'It was'ne me!' the poor man replied, but his sharp, dour wife didn't believe him and Will and Serena looked at each other, hands over their mouths.

'It's the pitch-pine pew – it made it echo!' Will whispered and they could barely stifle their laughter, prompting Will to fart again, much to their hilarity.

Soon, however, their high spirits were quelled by the vicar tapping Serena on the shoulder.

'Erm, I believe you're Luna's sister?' he asked. 'Could I have a word in private?' He wafted a service sheet in front of his nose.

'Of course,' replied Serena, hopping up before Stephanie noticed what was going on. She followed the vicar into his vestry.

'What's happened?' asked Serena. 'Don't tell me Luna hasn't turned up?'

'No, no, she's here, she's just arrived. She and your uncle are waiting in the porch. The problem is . . .' He took a deep breath. 'The bridegroom seems to have disappeared.'

'Seb? But I've seen him. He was here five minutes ago.'

'Indeed he was, but the best man is currently frantically searching for him. He said he was going outside for a cigarette, but now there's no sign of him. Do you have his number? Could you possibly give him a call?'

'Sure,' replied Serena, hunting for the mobile in her clutch bag. She located it and immediately dialled Seb's number.

'Voicemail,' she explained the next moment to the vicar, feeling a blind panic beginning to envelop her. 'Shit,' she said, and the vicar thought the language quite acceptable in the circumstances.

꩜

In the first month after the fateful wedding day, Luna had barely emerged from her bed. It had taken Serena a week to track Seb down and find out why he'd done it. She'd resorted to emulating a detective she'd seen on TV and spent an entire day crouched down low in her car outside Seb's block of flats until her patience paid off and he returned. She hopped out of the car and followed him in, confronting him in the communal hallway.

'You'd better come up,' he said, and Serena scurried along behind him up three flights of stairs.

'Would you like a coffee, tea or anything?' he asked, ever the gentleman. Serena couldn't help noticing how unkempt both he and the flat were looking. He was clearly suffering just as much as Luna.

'Why did you do it?' she asked a few minutes later, blowing on her tea. It was black, as Seb had nothing in his fridge, not even milk.

Seb sighed and slumped onto the armchair opposite Serena, as though his body was too heavy to keep upright for very long.

'It was the night before the wedding,' he began. 'I was feeling fine. Not too nervous. Well, a little anxious about being part of a big event, but not too nervous about the marriage itself although perhaps, if I'm honest, there had been a tiny seed of doubt. You know what a bridezilla Luna had been about the wedding and she'd been pretty vicious about some of my family – she wouldn't even let me invite my cousin Jenna. Took offence at something she said. Anyway, I was hopeful Luna would calm down after the big day, but let's just say I had a few concerns. We were having the night apart, as tradition dictates. Well, you know all this. She stayed with her friend Claudia; I was here. I thought I'd get an early night, so I ordered a takeaway and was about to settle down to watch *Prison Break* when the doorbell went.

'I answered it and who do you think was at the door? Your mum. I was more than surprised, as she'd never even been round here before. I don't know how she found me. Anyway, I invited her in. Offered her a drink. She was clearly agitated and I wondered if she thought Luna was making a mistake marrying me. So I tried to reassure her. I love Luna, I'm going to make her happy, etc., etc.

'But, "*I'm not worried about her,*" she said. "*It's you I'm concerned about. You don't know her. Not the real Luna. She can be ruthless. Somebody needs to tell you the truth. I hope you'll still go ahead tomorrow, but it's important you know what she did.*" And then she told me. About Freddie.'

Serena felt physically sick – her mouth dry, her heart pounding.

'What did she say?' she asked, her tongue feeling too large for her mouth.

'That he was your first boyfriend. You were madly in love with him. Brought him home from Majorca, only to have Luna seduce him. Not because she liked him, but just because she didn't want you to have him. It's true, isn't it?'

'Well, yes, it is . . . But I don't understand. Mum never knew. We kept it from her.'

'Well, either she worked it out at the time or Luna has told her since, but she knows alright. After that, she left. I gave myself a talking to. It's all long ago, she was only eighteen – all of that stuff. I didn't sleep well but I turned up at the church the next day. I was going to marry her regardless. But then I saw you. I saw you in the church, laughing with Will, and I thought to myself, I can't do this. I can't marry someone who would do that to her sister. Perhaps it was the final straw for me, after the way she'd been acting in the lead-up to the wedding. So I pretended to go for a fag and I legged it. I'm so sorry. I feel terrible. I should have at least had it out with her. I was a coward. And I do love her, I really do. But I can't be with someone like that. I just can't.'

Serena gave him a hug, then disappeared back to her car, her head spinning. She felt dreadful, for in a way she felt responsible though, of course, she knew that it was Luna who was the guilty party really. And yet it had been years now. Luna had changed. And now she had truly paid. She knew Seb was heartbroken but resolute. The love of Luna's life would not be walking back into her life, thanks to Stephanie. What could have possessed her to do that to her daughter? It was so out of character, for ordinarily she'd have been far more concerned about what her friends would think of a runaway bridegroom than anything else.

Serena sighed and turned on the engine. She would have to explain it all to Luna and pick up the pieces. *Blood is thicker than water*, she said to herself. And, at that moment, she realised. She had forgiven Luna. It may have taken a while, but she'd got there in the end.

The following day the girls confronted Stephanie, a united front. A terrible row ensued, with Stephanie claiming she'd had Luna's best interests at heart, that she'd believed Luna needed to start the marriage with everything out in the open. She was against divorce, she said: it was essential for everyone to take those solemn vows having laid their cards on the table.

Luna, perhaps understandably, told her in no uncertain terms that if anyone was going to be honest with Seb it should have been her and that Stephanie should have at least given her the choice. In the end, Stephanie apologised, admitting she'd never expected Seb to finish with Luna as a result and, after a while, relations were restored – to a point. But Luna was a shadow of her former self and Serena found herself almost wishing that a part of the old Luna – the funny, loud and bold part – would come back again. She missed her.

23.
AUGUST 2015

It was a Friday in August, a grey day more suited to autumn than summer, and Serena had decided to clean the Vicarage from top to toe. The boiler was working properly now and Max had finished all his painting, decorating and odd jobs in the house. It was all looking greatly refreshed and it seemed wrong not to get the whole place sparkling and gleaming as a finishing touch. It would be a good distraction from her various worries as well, which had not abated. She was still determined to take a proactive approach and find out more about the curse, but, feeling as though she had few allies in the village at the moment, she wasn't sure where to begin.

It was Mrs Pipe's day for helping and she arrived full of complaints about her other employers, the Smythes. Serena had never met them but she'd gleaned an awful lot about Mr Smythe, who was a miser, and Mrs Smythe, who thought herself 'bettermost' (in other words, superior) and was, in Mrs Pipe's opinion, 'chuckleheaded' (a most amusing term for stupid and one Serena would remember for future reference).

'Going under an operation today, Mrs Smythe is,' Mrs Pipe told her as she located her cleaning equipment. 'Women's troubles,' she added darkly. 'Gave Mr Smythe a dish of tongues, she did, when he couldn't find her best nightie to take up the hospital. I knew where it was; he always was a useless devil.'

The poor Smythes dealt with, Serena and Mrs Pipe began in the attic and didn't rest until even the scullery was shining bright and clean. Up in the attic everywhere was now freshly painted and a couple of the rooms contained neatly stacked boxes of the kind of useless possessions that get lugged from house to house for reasons of sentimentality. The largest attic room was a hive of activity, now being a small factory for Ashna's beautiful scarves and bedspreads. A table was in the centre of the room and on this stood a sewing machine and a swathe of ethnic material, all bright pinks and purples with jewels shimmering along the hemline. An upright chair was pulled up to the sewing table, but in the corner of the room was a much more cosy-looking armchair on which Ashna was sitting at this moment, stitching away as she listened to Radio 2.

'How's it all going?' asked Serena, handing Ashna a mug of tea as she always did mid-morning.

'Good, thanks. Trying to get an order ready for the shop. There's masses to do,' she explained. 'Ouch!' she exclaimed, as she jabbed the needle into her finger.

'We're distracting you,' said Serena. 'We'll leave you to it. We're just inspecting each room and deciding what needs sorting to get everything looking perfect. But it's as clean as anything in here.'

'I've got to keep it clean, so the material can be draped anywhere without getting dirty. Do you need my help?' she asked, about to abandon her work so she could assist.

'No.' Serena was definite. 'The two of us will get the place shining in no time, won't we, Mrs Pipe?'

Mrs Pipe nodded. 'Oh, aye, you've made the place a home,' she told Serena. 'Cherry on the top, to give it all a good clean now it's decorated. Got a nice feel to the place now, it has, despite . . .

you know, the curse,' she whispered, and Serena briskly moved the conversation on.

'Thank you, Mrs Pipe. Now, could I ask you to get started on the bathrooms, and I'll set about the bedrooms.' They left Ashna behind, descending the stairs to the first floor.

Mrs Pipe immediately began to scrub the bathroom, while Serena started polishing all the furniture in the master bedroom – even dusting along the skirting boards. She had the discretion not to enter Pete's or Ashna's bedrooms, however, and she decided on a very cursory clean of the nursery. The room increasingly unnerved her and it wasn't as though it was being used, after all.

Downstairs she began polishing every surface and giving everywhere a general tidy-up. She eventually slumped onto one of the sofas in the study and checked her watch. One o'clock. Lunchtime. She would make a salad for everyone in a moment, before sprucing up the kitchen in the afternoon, but for now she sank into the cushions and surveyed her surroundings.

It was definitely the homeliest reception room, with two cream settees scattered with colourful cushions (an idle Paddington stretched across one of them). A battered pine chest served as a coffee table and the fireplace was the central feature in the room, a landscape of the Sussex Downs hanging above it, given to Will by a grateful artist he'd helped in London during the final months of his life.

Some occasional tables were dotted here and there, and various lamps gave a cosy glow to the room as soon as evening descended. The back wall of the study was filled with books – both Will and Serena were voracious readers – and in one corner, beneath one of the windows, was Will's desk.

Giving Paddington one last tickle under her chin, and one last sniff – she loved how Paddington always seemed to smell of washing powder, thanks to her habit of snuggling up in freshly laundered linen – Serena heaved herself up and began vacuuming the rug in the hall until the Hoover began to make an alarming noise, then conked out altogether.

'Damn!' Serena knelt down to inspect it and realised the bag was full. She took it out of the inside cavity and went to the hall cupboard to find a replacement. Typically, they'd run out.

'What are you looking for?' asked Ashna, appearing in the hall.

'Hoover bags. We've run out and they don't sell them in the village. I'll have to nip into Rye later.'

'I'll go, if you like. Take the bus in.'

At this moment, Pete arrived in the hall as well. 'I'm starvin',' he said. 'Shall I make a start on lunch?'

'Yes, please. I'm making a bacon and avocado salad,' Serena told him. 'Actually, Pete, would you mind driving Ashna into Rye this afternoon? You can take my car. We need Hoover bags.'

Ashna and Pete looked at each other and smiled.

'Sure, of course,' Pete replied, before dashing downstairs to the kitchen. Serena wondered if they were onto her. She was always sending them off on little errands and clearly it didn't take two people to buy Hoover bags, although it would be much easier to take the car than the bus. Anyway, they seemed happy enough with the outcome.

Once lunch had been served and eaten, Serena and Mrs Pipe began on the kitchen and all its annexes and by the end of the afternoon, everywhere felt entirely cleansed. It was a shame, thought Serena, it wouldn't stay like it. But still, it had been incredibly cathartic. She showered, washing away all the grime and dust, but still felt surprisingly energetic, and decided to round the day off with a cycle ride through the village. The day, uninspiring, had turned into a beautiful evening: pink clouds in a purple sky.

She cycled past the church and pub and along the high street, breathing in the scent of freesias and foliage as she passed the florist's, waving at Bob the butcher and the Colonel, collecting his paper. She picked up speed past the health centre and turned right up the hill towards the station. At the railway line, the lights were flashing so she hopped off her pushbike and stood and waited patiently as the red-and-white gates slowly descended. A minute passed until she heard the lines crackle and the next moment the fast train to London swept by at high speed, leaving a not unpleasant smell of diesel in its wake.

The gates opened again and Serena jumped back on the bike. She pedalled her way laboriously to the top of the hill and, there at the summit, turned and paused to look down on the village beneath her. From this viewpoint Serena could see the church in the distance and the roof of the Vicarage, the thatches of the cottages just beyond the pub and the parched, yellowed grass of the playing fields. She had a good view of the high street too, and she marvelled at how long the shops must have been in existence – the village was ancient although, while the building that housed the grocer's was old, it was unlikely to have been called 'CostKutter' in years gone by.

It was such a lovely parish, thought Serena: just the right size, with all the charm and convenience you could wish for, so that there was little need ever to venture out of the place. She just hoped that they could win the villagers round.

This thought reminded her that it was the first youth club session that evening and she decided to poke her head in to see how it was going. She had a few goosebumps now, the warmth of the day gone although it was not yet close to dark. She jumped back on the bike and raced down the hill, narrowly avoiding crashing into Miss Dawson ('Road hog!' she shouted; she was probably on her way to the Women's Institute at the community centre and did not look impressed at having to jump out of Serena's way). By the time Serena arrived at the church hall, she was pink in the face and much warmer again.

She dumped the bike outside the front and quietly opened the blue door, not wishing to disturb whatever was going on. It all seemed very peaceful. She peeked around, but couldn't see any kids at all. Nor Max and Ashna. It *was* Friday, wasn't it? She would just check the kitchen. Serena climbed the few steps up to the kitchen door. She opened it. And there, sitting on the worktop, was Ashna, her hands in Max's hair as they kissed.

Serena retreated quietly. They hadn't seen her. She crept out of the hall, gathered up her bike and walked with it along the lane and back to the Vicarage, feeling both shocked and delighted. So much for her matchmaking. She'd been so intent on getting Ashna and Pete together that she hadn't noticed a closeness developing between Ashna and Max, but, now she thought about it, it was perfect. Two gentle souls, who'd each been treated so badly in the past, finding solace in each other.

Arriving back at the Vicarage, she found Pete making tea in the kitchen and told him what she'd just observed, admitting she'd been hoping to pair up Ashna with him. He laughed.

'We had noticed! Serena, I always had you down as pretty observant. You know, Ashna is a beautiful girl, but hadn't you realised? I'm gay,' he told her.

'Are you?' she asked, surprised for the second time in a quarter of an hour. 'But you don't *seem* very gay,' she told him.

'Will warned us about you and your stereotypin',' he chuckled in reply.

'I feel ashamed,' she told him, anxiously twisting her curls around her finger. 'Not only about that, but it's just occurred to me that in trying to matchmake you two, I was no better than Ashna's family, trying to force her into a marriage.'

Pete put down his mug. 'It's hardly the same thing,' he replied, putting out his arms. 'I think we can safely say you had good intentions . . . Now, come 'ere,' he said, 'and give me a cuddle.'

24.
SUMMER 2012

Unfortunately, Serena was one of the unlucky ones whose quiet disorder did not seem to respond to medication or nutritional adaptations. A gluten-free diet – combined with the right drugs – had been almost certain to cure the problem, leaving her consultant flummoxed. He couldn't be sure now whether the infertility was connected to the coeliac disease or whether the diagnosis had been a red herring and Serena was simply a victim of the dreaded 'unexplained infertility'. Either way, the result was the same. No baby. Nine years and three rounds of IVF later, Serena and Will had just about given up on their dream of having a baby.

Serena hadn't been the only one having a tough time of it either – after being jilted at the altar, Luna had spiralled into a pit of despair. The only silver lining was that she and Serena became close at last, joined in their mutual misfortune. And Serena had been there for Luna when she made the mistake of jumping into a rebound relationship with a steroid-addicted, body-building thug called Phil, who spent two years being heavy with his fists. He wasn't clever enough to keep his violence hidden, or perhaps he didn't care, so Luna always seemed to be wearing sunglasses to hide her bruised eyes. Serena and Will despaired, constantly trying to encourage Luna to leave him. When Serena found Luna self-harming one evening, as if she wasn't enduring enough harm from Phil, she decided enough was enough. She packed up Luna's belongings and moved her into the curate's house in Hither Green, where she nursed her sister's physical and emotional injuries, insisting on paying for her to have several counselling sessions in an effort to rebuild Luna's paper-thin self-esteem.

The counselling helped and Luna's moods seemed to stabilise over the following seven years. She'd sworn off men, but threw herself into her job as a journalist and spent every spare moment doing charity work at the local Women's Refuge, where the stories she heard, even worse than her own, were enough to put her off men for life. It seemed that in assisting women less fortunate than herself, she'd found some peace at last.

When Will and Serena moved to a bungalow in Lewisham, where Will had been promoted to the role of vicar at St Mary's, Luna found herself a flat just two streets away from them so they got together as often as their busy schedules would allow. Occasionally Serena tried to set Luna up with a stray bachelor, organising dinner parties at which she would place her sister next to the man in question and would eye them beadily from the other end of the table.

But Luna was determined. She didn't need a man. She would flirt, of course. That part of her was inbuilt, but any hopes she raised were quickly dashed when she failed to reply to texts or phone calls in the days and weeks that followed.

And although there were still hints of Luna's moodiness now, it seemed that as she'd matured she'd certainly learned to deal with her temperament better.

She was actually very funny, although usually at the cost of others. Luna often joined Serena and Will for evenings in front of the television and had them both in stitches with her acerbic comments about the actors or presenters. Poor Nigella Lawson was one of her victims.

'This cake is just oozing with sex appeal, don't you think?' Luna would ask, looking up mock-coyly from under her eyelashes. 'Look at me, devouring it in the middle of the night like the saucy insomniac I am!'

Facebook was great fodder for Luna's caustic commentary, as well. She would sit on the sofa with her laptop and look up old school friends, making retching noises as she read out their posts.

'*Feeling so blessed to have the best hubbie in the world and the cutest kids ever!*' she would read out. 'They look like demons to me. Look, Serena, don't you agree?' She would pass the computer to Serena, who would cast her eye at a photo of two entirely blameless-looking little faces.

'They look blessedly cute to me,' she would giggle, and Luna would tut and move onto her next victim.

Serena, meanwhile, was coming to terms with remaining childless. Unlike Will, who was sick and tired of attempting to become a parent, she hadn't *quite* got there. Various kindly friends asked whether they might consider adoption, but the thought of that lengthy and difficult process after all they'd been through already didn't really appeal.

'We'll get a dog,' said Will.

'Maybe,' Serena would say in reply. But they hadn't got one so far. She had, however, picked up some holiday brochures. One summer evening, as she and Will drank Pimm's in their tiny back garden, listening to the sirens of ambulances dashing back and forth to the nearby hospital, she showed them to him.

'What are these?' Will asked, flicking through the pile.

'A trip. What do you think? I thought Australia. We could maybe visit Lisa and Todd in Perth and the Davidsons in Sydney. Hire a camper van and travel around for a little while?'

'Now, that would be amazing!' smiled Will. 'How long for? A month maybe?'

'Yes, I thought a month if we're going that far. Just think: no responsibilities, no parishioners, no work, no chores – for four whole weeks. And sunshine too – wall-to-wall sunshine.'

'Oh, Serena, that's a fabulous idea! The only problem is money . . . We're totally broke after the IVF . . .'

'We've got the inheritance from my Dad, remember . . . I've kept it tucked away. It's been sitting in the bank in case of emergencies, but how much better to use it for something truly memorable? I think we should be able to do the trip and have some left over as well. Shall we book it for next November, so we have ages to save and plan and look forward to it?'

'Definitely!' Will agreed. He wondered if this meant what he hoped it meant.

'A new chapter in our lives,' Serena said, as if reading his mind. 'Just us. Not so bad, hey, after all,' she smiled, nudging him. Will took her hand.

'Just us.'

25.
SEPTEMBER 2015

Serena had just stepped out of the shower (glorious hot water, any time of day, now the boiler was reliable) when she heard the phone ringing. She shrugged on her dressing gown and lunged for the bedroom extension.

'Vicarage,' she said.

'Hello, Vicarage, it's Alice. Are you free tomorrow night? Terribly short notice, I know, but I'm hosting a house-warming party.'

Serena sat down on her bed. 'House-warming? Alice, what are you talking about? You've lived in your house for years.'

'Darling, I've left him.'

'What? But when? You didn't say anything last weekend!'

'I know, I wanted it to be a *fait accompli* before I told anyone, including *him*. I'm renting a furnished house on the estate next to the health centre. I've never lived in a new build and it's a revelation. So warm and snug. Serena, I feel so happy – liberated. That's why I've decided to throw a party. I need to celebrate.'

'Well, good on you! And how about the kids? Are they okay? And Rob?'

'The kids are fine – enjoying the novelty and being able to scoot around the estate with the other children. And Rob is in bits. He honestly never thought I'd leave him. I gave him good reason to think he could have his cake and eat it, but enough's enough. He can set up with Tanya now if he wants. She's welcome to him!'

'Alice, you're so brave to have done it. I'm so impressed. And of course we'll come tomorrow. Who else will be there?'

'Oh, you know, various friends from the village. You'll see. It's just drinks, from seven. See you tomorrow!'

'Bye,' replied Serena, but Alice had already rung off, presumably to ring the next person on her list.

❦

Serena was just applying a little lip gloss in the hall mirror before the party when she was accosted by Ashna.

'Serena, have you got a minute?' she asked. She was dressed in skinny black jeans and a pink tunic dress, her long dark hair shiny, her eyes clear and bright. She looked stunning.

'Of course,' Serena replied, smacking her lips together. 'What is it?'

'Well, you know nobody came to the first youth club?' she started. Serena nodded, smiling inwardly. 'Well, the thing is that Max and I ended up chatting and before we knew it, we were kissing, and . . . Oh, Serena, I'm totally mad about him. I just had to tell you. We said we'd keep it quiet for now, but I need to talk to someone about it. He's in my head all the time,' she said, the picture of a dreamy young girl in love.

'I know,' Serena giggled. 'I caught you kissing! But you didn't notice me so I skulked off.'

Ashna blushed. 'How embarrassing!' she laughed. 'But isn't he just divine? Isn't he just the most gorgeous man you've ever seen?'

'Very tasty,' agreed Serena. 'Though you might have noticed, I'm partial to a redhead myself. But the two of you are perfect together. If you ever have children, they'll be the most beautiful creatures on the planet. Here he comes now,' she finished with a whisper, hearing Max's distinctive singing as he emerged from the kitchen stairwell (he always seemed to be singing since he and Ashna had got together).

'You've told her, haven't you?' he laughed, seeing their guilty faces.

'I couldn't help it,' confessed Ashna, and they were instantly drawn towards each other.

'I'm just so pleased,' Serena told them. 'And it was about time something good happened . . . There seems to have been so much stress recently with one thing or another. Do you think we'll be snubbed by anyone at the party tonight?'

'I'm sure Alice is a seasoned hostess,' said Max. 'She won't have invited anyone who'd be hostile to you and Will. And we have you to thank, actually, for getting us together.'

'Really? But I definitely didn't matchmake you. I was planning to get Ashna together with Pete!' Serena confessed.

Max laughed. 'But you listened to me. That day of the fete, when I had that breakdown and I told you about all the awful stuff that had happened with Lara. I'd been bottling it all up inside, not dealing with it. I'd moved on in so many ways, but I didn't think I'd ever be ready for another relationship. Offloading to you that day, it was cathartic. And it made me realise that I was ready. And fortunately, Ashna seems to feel the same way about me as I do about her,' he added, his arm around her. 'Thank you,' Max said to Serena in a more serious tone.

'You're welcome!' replied Serena. 'I really couldn't be happier for you both. Now,' she said, putting away her lip gloss, 'we really ought to go or we'll be late. Where's Will?'

On cue, Will appeared from the study. 'Sorry, just been finishing tomorrow's sermon so I can let my hair down tonight. What about Pete?'

'He's going to meet us there.'

'Come on then, let's go!'

∽

The house was lovely: miles smaller than Alice's Georgian pile but very cosy and welcoming, far less minimalist in fact, and there were signs that Alice might be cutting herself some slack too – piles of laundry ready to go upstairs, unplumped cushions, untidy kitchen surfaces. She even looked a little more relaxed in her appearance, her hair wavy instead of ironed poker straight, and her make-up more natural. She looked years younger.

'Come in, come in,' she welcomed, ushering them through to the sitting room. 'Now, what would you all like to drink? There's Prosecco, wine, beer . . .' They all placed different orders so Will went through to the kitchen with Alice to assist, while the others joined the merry throng already well and truly into the swing of the party. Max and Ashna immediately spotted Pete and Jake Hardy and went over to chat to them, and Serena, spying the Colonel sitting alone on a sofa, went to join him. He was smoking his pipe and Alice seemed remarkably relaxed about the distinctive, sweet smoke filling her sitting room.

'Hello, Colonel,' Serena said, greeting him with a kiss.

'Hello there, dear. Audrey, isn't it?' he asked. 'Sorry, terrible at remembering names these days.'

'Oh, don't worry at all, but it's Serena,' she said.

'Yes, thought it was. Lovely to see you, Audrey.'

Serena tried not to laugh, accepting her drink from Will, who was then accosted by Bob the butcher. They chatted for a few moments before Will disappeared back to the kitchen.

'Came from London, didn't you? How are you finding village life? Not too dull?' the Colonel asked, taking a sip of brandy.

'I love it. I grew up in a village nearby so it's not such a culture shock for me. We're a little upset though that the villagers don't seem to be taking to us,' she admitted.

'Yes, you seem to be settling in splendidly. As though you've always been here, part of the village,' the Colonel replied, nodding. It seemed the cacophony of chatter and laughter from the other guests was playing havoc with his hearing. She recalled Mrs Pipe telling her recently, and rather alarmingly, that the Colonel was '*afflicted with deathness, poor codger*'. Serena had asked if he was unwell and Mrs Pipe had replied, to Serena's relief, that he was '*well enough, but thick of hearing*'.

'I'll tell you what, Colonel,' said Serena directly into his ear. 'Shall we go and have a look at the garden? Such a beautiful evening.'

'Cracking idea. You might need to help heave me up though. Hope you don't mind.'

'Of course not,' Serena replied and she pulled him up off the sofa using his only arm. He reached for his glass and, with his pipe clamped between his teeth, the two of them went through the kitchen and into the utility room.

The door to the garden was slightly ajar and Serena was about to push it open when she heard Will's voice on the other side.

'She thinks the bloody house is cursed,' he was saying. 'It's so ridiculous. I don't know what's got into her. We could do without that on top of the problems in the village.' Serena, frozen to the spot, felt tears spring to her eyes. She wasn't sure who Will was talking to, but this wasn't like him. He was usually so loyal. She must really have got to him, for him to be letting off steam like this about her. Enough was enough.

'Come along then,' barked the Colonel, held up behind her.

'Actually, Colonel, how about we take a seat in the kitchen – at that little table over there. It's nice and quiet. There's something I need to ask you about.'

'Righto,' he agreed and, once ensconced, she began.

'Do you know about the curse on the Vicarage?' she asked him, getting straight to the point.

'Ah, yes, that story's been around a long time. Certainly since I've been in the village. Thirty years. Worried about it, are you?' he asked, and Serena realised the Colonel was more perceptive than he might at first seem.

'It's bothering me. I get a funny feeling in the nursery. And I can't get it out of my head. Ever since Mrs Pipe told me, I can't stop thinking about it.'

'Silly woman, telling you. That was a mistake.'

'Is it true though?' Serena asked. 'Is it true that a baby hasn't lived at the Vicarage since the vicar's wife died at the turn of the last century?'

'Well, there's not been a baby born into the Vicarage since I've been here, but as I say, that's only thirty years. Tell you what. I'm a keen historian. Always have been. I could do with a project. Keep me busy. Why don't you let me look into it for you? See what I can find out about the curse, the history . . . Would that help?'

'Oh, it would,' Serena told him, hugging him. 'It really would.'

'Steady on, old girl,' the Colonel replied. 'Here, you couldn't just get me a refill, could you?' he asked, proffering his glass.

Serena jumped up. 'Of course,' she told him, beaming as she located the brandy bottle. This was it. The Colonel was on the case. She felt a great sense of relief. Her proactive approach had begun.

After their conversation, the Colonel made his excuses and left the party and Serena tracked down Alice.

'Come on, time to tell me all the goss,' she said, while they settled down together on a sofa with a bottle of wine. Alice explained about her carefully planned departure while gentle music played in the background and a hum of chatter surrounded them.

'So has he gone off with Tanya then?' Serena asked.

'Ha! Well, that's the funny thing. Jake has left her too – he's staying at some ghastly B & B down the road, poor thing. So *she's* on her own and Rob's on *his* own. But guess what? They're not interested in each other now there's no cloak and dagger about it all.'

'Will you go back to him?' Serena asked.

'Do you know, I thought I would. Thought I'd just teach him a lesson. But now I'm not so sure . . . I feel like a different person. A better person. I'm not sure I want to go back. Anyway, we'll see. Good heavens, what on earth's that banging? Hang on a sec.' Alice hopped up from the sofa and answered the door.

'Miss Dawson!' Alice said next. 'Do come in!'

'I'm not here to join the debauchery,' she told Alice. Serena found the iPod and turned the music from low to mute. 'I am here to give you an official warning as leader of the neighbourhood watch for this area. We do *not* have parties that last long into the night around here. And we do *not* disturb each other or cause a nuisance of any kind. Do you understand, or would you like me to involve the police?' Miss Dawson asked, her wattle wobbling with indignation.

'Golly, I'm awfully sorry. I didn't think we were being terribly loud. I shall send everyone on their way,' Alice promised her. Miss Dawson looked slightly taken aback, if not a little disappointed. Serena suspected she'd been rather looking forward to a good fight.

'Right. Well. Much obliged,' she announced, before turning on her stout heel and returning home. Unfortunately for Alice, she lived directly opposite.

Alice shut the door, checked her watch and returned to her guests.

'Well, I'm sorry to tell you that it's time you all left. It's far later than you'd probably imagined. I know you're not going to believe this but – wait for it – it's a quarter past nine!'

Everyone burst out laughing, but the party was over, and they drained the remains of their drinks, collected their coats and, after no doubt a little too much in the way of raucous outdoor goodbyes, the guests headed home.

26.
DECEMBER 2013

By the time Will and Serena reached Perth on a balmy afternoon in December, they'd journeyed all over Australia by plane, bus and camper van. They arrived at Perth airport exhausted, filthy and extremely happy.

They took a cab to Lisa and Todd's house in the suburbs, where Serena was amazed to see that utter chaos reigned. Lisa had always been incredibly neat and tidy at university, but it seemed the addition of a new baby had caused havoc in the household. Tess was only three weeks old and Serena and Will had offered to stay at a hotel rather than imposing on their friends when they had a newborn, but Lisa had been insistent they should stay.

'You're here!' Todd grinned, pulling Will and Serena into a hug. 'Sorry the house is a tip, but the nipper's causing mayhem. But look, if you don't mind the mess we're just so pleased to have you here. Just make yourselves at home! You interested in the cricket? I've got it on. Have a tinny,' he said, handing a beer to Will and another to Serena, who smiled appreciatively. 'Don't worry about your bags. I'll take them to your room in a mo. Too easy.' Todd was still the affable, easy-going guy she remembered from all those years ago when she'd met him on her course and then, later, fixed him up with Lisa.

'Where's Lisa?' Serena asked, wondering where her friend had got to. Ordinarily, Lisa would have been bouncing around her, greeting her with great enthusiasm.

'Oh, sorry, mate, she's just having a nap. She didn't get any sleep last night and she finally got the baby off about an hour ago so she's taking advantage. She wanted me to wake her up. Let me get her.'

'No, don't!' Serena told him, stopping him. 'Let her sleep. How's Tess?'

'Oh, she's gorgeous but, boy, does she have a pair of lungs on her. Hope you've brought earplugs with you,' he grinned. 'Come and take a load off while the girls sleep, Serena. You'll soon see. You need to rest when you can in this house.'

He wasn't wrong. By eight o'clock, Lisa had emerged from her bedroom, appalled she'd missed her friends' arrival. Lisa looked incredibly dishevelled – her hair all rumpled, no make-up and wearing some crumpled old nightie, but she still looked as pretty as she ever had. Prettier, perhaps, despite the lack of sleep, with her Australian suntan and post-baby glow.

Tess had woken for a feed at around nine, before obligingly going to sleep in Serena's arms (she'd managed to place her back in her Moses basket without waking her up), and the four of them had enjoyed a civilised evening on the veranda, eating a takeaway, Will and Serena marvelling at the late-night warmth. They'd had so much to catch up on that it was late by the time they all got to bed – nearly midnight. Serena had just been drifting off when Tess began to cry. She was definitely a creature of the night.

Will and Serena lay there all night, listening to the hushed, desperate sounds of their friends trying to get the baby to go off again. They drifted into sleep intermittently, but were repeatedly woken by her sharp cries.

The next morning everyone sat around the breakfast table looking sorry for themselves.

'Colic, the doctor says,' Lisa told Serena gloomily as she held the baby in her arms. It was boiling so Tess was just wearing a nappy. 'Doctor says it might last three months. I honestly think I'll have died of sleep-deprivation by then.' There was a loud noise and everyone looked at the baby appalled, as poo erupted from the nappy and seeped down Tess's legs and all down Lisa's nightie.

'Oh, grand,' said Lisa, about to get up.

'Let me do it,' Serena said, taking Tess from her friend. 'You go and shower.'

'Are you sure?'

'Of course.'

Later, sitting in the shade on the veranda as the men mucked about in the pool and Tess slept in her Moses basket, Lisa looked at her friend.

'How are you feeling now?' she asked. 'You know, about the whole baby thing. You've had a flippin' rough time of it. I was a bit worried about you coming to stay. I hope it's not too painful, being around a baby.'

'It's been horrendous,' Serena told her. 'A strain on us as a couple, as well. But this trip has been so healing. And you needn't worry. It's just wonderful to have this time with Tess, but also to be able to hand her back.'

'It's not all it's cracked up to be, you know. I love that baby to bits, but it's like we're trying to survive some kind of hurricane that's hit the house.'

'It'll get easier,' Serena assured her friend. 'It's a big change. You'll be loving it within a month or two, I bet.'

Lisa smiled weakly. 'Yeah, well, we'll see, hey. But it's tough . . . Really tough.'

'You're doing great,' Serena said, recognising Lisa was in dire need of some reassurance. 'You're a brilliant mum. A natural.'

'I'm so glad you're here, pet,' Lisa said, squeezing her hand.

By the time it came for them to leave, Serena realised that – rather than being painful – staying with Lisa, Todd and Tess had been a cure of sorts. It had made Serena realise that having a baby wasn't a bed of roses. Of course, if she'd had a choice, she'd still have rather had one than not, but she'd seen first-hand that it wasn't necessarily all it was cracked up to be, as Lisa had said. And, at last, for Serena and Will it was no longer the be-all and end-all.

❧

They arrived back from Australia just before Christmas to find Luna in a state of high excitement.

'Can I come round tonight?' she asked on the phone, just hours after they'd returned. They were feeling enormously jetlagged and travel weary, but Luna was clearly desperate to see them so they agreed and decided to delay their unpacking and all hopes of an early night. Will nipped to the local shop to buy some ingredients for supper and a bottle of wine, while Serena stacked up the pile of unread post, turned up the heating and dashed around putting on lamps.

'Oh my goodness, look at you both! So tanned and healthy-looking. How was it? Did you have a great time? Isn't it freezing here?' Luna greeted them both with kisses, which left red lip-shaped marks on their cheeks, and the entire room was suffused in her signature scent, a perfume that would be overpowering on most people, but that Luna was somehow able to get away with.

'It was wonderful,' Serena told her. 'It went in a flash and yet it seems ages since we left. Let me show you the photos,' she continued, grabbing her phone and Luna sat down next to Serena on the sofa and made all the right noises about the Great Ocean Road, the Sydney Opera House and Serena cuddling koalas. Eventually, supper was served.

'Food's up,' said Will and they gathered around the kitchen table for Thai chicken curry with rice and a green salad. Even under time pressure, Will seemed able to produce the most delicious meals.

'So, guys, I can't hold back any longer. I simply have to tell you the exciting news,' Luna announced as they tucked in.

'What is it?' smiled Serena. She imagined Luna must have found herself a new man at last.

'I've met this woman,' she explained, and Serena wondered if her sister had suddenly turned gay in the last month.

'Oh yes?'

'She's at the refuge. She's incredible. So inspiring. Anyway, she was in a terrible relationship but she has this amazing job. She advises people about surrogacy. So we got chatting and it came to me, out of the blue, just sitting there listening to her. I mean this with all my heart. Serena. Will. Let me be your surrogate.'

If she'd expected them to jump for joy and agree immediately, she'd have been mistaken. Will and Serena sat, shocked, at the table, forks poised in mid-air. They had just been on their watershed holiday and had finally come to terms with their situation after years of trying to conceive. And now Luna was offering them this?

'But Luna, do you know what you're saying here? You'd have to hand over the baby!' Serena said, her head instantly spinning.

'I know all that but it doesn't bother me in the least. I never wanted kids myself anyway. You know that. And the baby would be yours. I've learnt all about it. I remember you saying there's nothing wrong with either of you reproductively; it's just the getting pregnant that seems to be the trouble. So the baby would be genetically yours, and I'd just host the pregnancy. Okay, so it might involve a bit of sickness – and I don't much like being sick – but that would be the worst of it. Well, that and actually pushing the baby out, I suppose. But, hey, there are bound to be some pretty good painkillers, right?'

Serena was astonished. Luna was absolutely sincere. She was genuinely offering to do this for them.

'But what if you've got an autoimmune disorder too? We're identical twins, after all. I know the doctor can't be sure now that that's the problem, but still . . .'

'I got tested while you were away and luckily I haven't. That's how serious I am about this,' Luna told them. 'I really am.'

'Luna, this is amazing of you. So incredibly generous. But, as you know, the whole reason we went on the trip to Australia was because we've finally come to terms with never having children. We'll need to talk about it, think it through really carefully. Will?' she asked, turning to him, her eyes wide with fear and excitement.

'Luna, this is exceptionally kind of you. We'll certainly think about the offer, of course. But, as Serena says, we'd just accepted our situation, found some peace at last. To be honest, I'm nervous about allowing ourselves any further hope.'

'I totally understand,' replied Luna, her eyes bright. 'After all you've been through, you'd be mad to agree without finding out all the facts and thinking it all over. But look, the offer's there. And can I give you Zara's number so you can get some more information about it all? She said I could give it to you.'

'Of course,' said Will and he took the number from Luna and put it in his back pocket. 'And now, it looks like you're in need of a top-up,' he said, filling Luna's glass with wine.

'Thank you,' she said, and he and Serena toasted Luna.

'There's no rush,' Luna said. 'And I won't change my mind. Just think about it . . .'

'We will,' Serena told her. 'We will.' She tried to take a mouthful of food, but found her appetite lost. She could hardly believe it. *One last chance?* she wondered. She had no idea what Will was thinking, but she knew this was an offer she was going to find hard to refuse.

27.
SEPTEMBER 2015

Serena was sulking, not that Will had noticed. He was too busy preparing for the morning's service.

'I'm not going to church today,' Serena told him as she lay in bed while Will dressed, slipping his dog collar over his black clerical shirt.

'Okey dokey. I'll probably nip into the pub for a sharpener after the service. Could you put the chicken in at about twelve?'

'Sure,' she replied, curt, but Will dashed off, oblivious.

'See you later!' he called.

Serena lay back on the goose-down pillows and thought about the previous evening. She recalled she'd left the party in reasonable spirits, but she'd woken this morning remembering Will talking about her behind her back and felt quite put out about it now that she had time to dwell. But it was no good moping: she would have to confront him.

Fortunately, it was just the two of them for lunch as Max had taken Ashna to meet his family and Pete was helping Jake Hardy move a few more bits and pieces out of the farmhouse and into the local B & B.

They chatted about this and that over the roast, but as Serena dished out raspberries for their pudding she tackled Will about the conversation she'd overheard.

'I don't know who it was, but you were moaning about me to someone. Saying I was obsessed about the house being cursed,' Serena said, hurt.

'I'm sorry,' Will said, instantly contrite. 'That was bad of me. If it makes it any better, I was just letting off steam to Alice. But, Serena, it's just that I'm worried about you. I want you to be able to put everything that happened behind you now and start afresh. I can't bear you to fixate on something so superstitious when we need to be starting again.'

'But what if it's true, Will? The curse. I've asked the Colonel about it. He's going to look into it all for me.'

'Why are you wasting his time, Serena? It's all just nonsense!' Will was agitated now, his patience wearing thin.

'Have you given up, Will? Is that it? We must never give up,' she told him, her cheeks an angry red. 'I'm still hoping. And you should be too.'

'Serena, there *is* no hope.' There. He'd said it. Will looked at her, no longer cross – instead sad but stern. It was about time he said it aloud, perhaps as much to convince himself as Serena.

Serena threw the raspberries at him and stormed out of the house, slamming the front door behind her.

Seething inwardly, Serena went for a walk or perhaps a stomp. She made her way down the high street, her face like thunder. Bob the butcher called out to her but she just waved briefly and carried on, hoping the exercise would dispel her anger. It didn't, so she decided to pause at the pub before heading home. She peered around the black stable door. Thankfully it wasn't very busy, just a few Sunday drinkers idling the afternoon away and no one she knew very well.

'You alright, love?' asked Tanya, spotting Serena at the bar. 'What can I get you?'

'A brandy, please,' Serena told her.

'Right you are. Here we go. That's three pounds twenty.' Serena rummaged in her pockets and handed over a five-pound note, then waited for the change.

She'd just found herself a discreet corner booth when her mobile began to ring. She thought it would be Will, but it was a number she didn't recognise.

'Hello?'

'Serena. It's Freddie!'

'Freddie! I can't believe it!'

'I've been trying to get hold of you for a while, Serena. In the end I tracked down your mum and she gave me your mobile.'

'But why are you calling? Is everything okay? Are the family alright?' asked Serena. She sipped her brandy. It warmed her heart and the heady mix of alcohol and an emotional day made her feel instantly tipsy.

'They're all well, thanks. Mum's started taking in rescue dogs so the farmhouse is more chaotic than ever. Dad's fine – had a health scare a year ago but he's okay now. And the girls are the same as ever – Amber and Ebs have got six kids between them now and you'll never guess what – Little Jane is a doctor!'

'No way! That teeny little kid, so sweet and unassuming. What kind of doctor?'

'A cardiologist no less! She's the success of the family. Surprised everyone, I think . . . And your family?' asked Freddie carefully. 'I didn't speak to your mum for long, but she did tell me about your father – I'm so sorry. He was such a gentleman.'

'Yes,' agreed Serena. 'Yes, he was.' She decided not to mention Luna. She wasn't sure where she'd begin. Instead: 'Freddie, why did you want me?'

'To apologise. I know, I know. It was a long time ago. But I've been eaten up with guilt for so long now that I just knew I had to call you. Serena, I've made some mistakes in my life, but sleeping with your sister was, without a doubt, the most stupid thing I've ever done. And I know I apologised at the time, but understandably you didn't want to hear it.'

Serena took another warming sip. 'But why now? I mean, it really was an age ago, Freddie.'

'Because now I know how it feels, Serena. I was given a healthy dose of karma. After we broke up, I went back to Majorca for a bit, then went off travelling. I felt like such a shit, so I made myself do the kind of travelling that's a bit tough – building an orphanage, helping to rehabilitate orangutans, trekking through the Himalayas. I think I was trying to prove I wasn't a complete bastard. Anyway, I met girls here and there, had a few flings, but nothing serious. Every woman I met made me feel emptier and lonelier than if I was on my own. They just couldn't match up to you.'

Serena tried not to feel too triumphant about this. 'So then what happened?' she asked.

'Then, eventually, I fell in love again, with a Spanish girl. I got married, had a gorgeous little baby boy. I was the happiest I'd been since . . . us. And then, last year, Valentina ran off with one of my friends. One of my best friends. And she took our little boy with her. He's just turned three. Now I'm lucky if I see Mateo once a month. I need to sort out better access, but it will never be the same again. I thought I had it all. But it was temporary. So fleeting. She broke my heart. And after that, I knew I had to speak to you. To tell you how sorry I am. That I know now how it feels.' There was a pause.

'Of course I forgive you, Freddie. You *did* break my heart and you *did* behave like a bastard. But it was a long time ago.'

'Oh, Serena, I'm so relieved. I thought you'd put the phone down on me and I'd have to spend the rest of my life feeling guilty.'

'Don't think any more about it, it's water under the bridge. But, Freddie, did you honestly call just to apologise for something that happened so long ago?'

'Well, no . . . There was something else. Serena, I keep thinking about you lately. Keep wondering how things might have turned out if I hadn't been such an idiot. I just wondered . . . Would you like to meet up? I'm in London right now. I don't know what your circumstances are, but . . .'

Listening to Freddie, hearing his melodious voice, it was strange. As if, all at once, the intervening years had never happened. She was eighteen again, in Deia, listening to Malcolm strumming 'Layla' on his guitar on a humid summer's night, while Freddie wrapped his arms around her and nuzzled into her long blonde hair.

She came back to the present with a start.

'Freddie, I'm in a relationship,' she told him.

28.
MARCH 2014

In the end, they decided to give the surrogacy one shot. Zara was a convincing advocate of the process. They met her at a coffee shop and she ran them through everything. They saw a lawyer, of course, who was clearly sceptical about the arrangement while more than content to take his fee. It probably did seem a bit mad to anyone other than the three of them and Zara, but Will and Serena had decided to give it just one chance – one last chance.

Stephanie certainly couldn't understand it. 'So how will it all work?' she asked, wrinkling her nose with distaste.

'It's quite simple really. Luna will be a host surrogate, which means she'll carry the baby, but genetically he or she will be ours: Will and I will create the embryo. Once the baby is six weeks old, Luna will give her consent for a parental order to be made in our favour so we'll make that application to the court, which might take a little while. There may need to be a hearing or two but once that's all sorted, the baby will be legally, as well as genetically, ours.'

'Well, it all sounds very unusual, but I'm sure you know what you're doing,' Stephanie said, making it clear she thought the exact opposite. Serena supposed it was going to be a difficult subject to explain to her friends. 'Isn't it dreadfully expensive?'

'It's not cheap, that's for sure. That's why we're only going to try it the once. We're using the rest of the money Dad left me. Look, Mum, you'll see,' Serena said, refusing to be put off. 'As soon as you've got your grandchild in your arms, you'll forget all about how he or she got here. That's what Zara keeps telling us.'

'Well, there's many a slip . . .' Stephanie started, but managed to stop herself, with obvious superhuman effort. 'I can hardly wait,' she changed tack. 'A grandchild. At long last. I'm the last of all my friends, you know.' Even that comment implied criticism, but Serena let it all wash over her. She was far too excited about getting started.

The process itself was not all that foreign to them. It mirrored the IVF process they'd already been through, but this time the twins went through the most stressful parts of it together: the egg-harvesting for Serena and, for her sister, implantation of the embryo.

Luna was remarkably uncomplaining about it all. She'd committed to it and she was going to see it through. Will and Serena were unspeakably grateful and fussed around her as though she were an invalid. In the two weeks following implantation, they dropped round to her flat with home-cooked meals and made sure she had her feet up in the evenings.

'You know, I bloody hope this has worked,' Luna joked. 'I'm going to be seriously cheesed off if I don't get to enjoy nine months of this pampering.'

After a very long fortnight, the day for the testing appointment arrived. It also happened to be Luna and Serena's birthday. The three of them were so nervous on the drive to the fertility clinic they could barely speak to each other. The doctor laughed when he saw them.

'I can almost smell the nerves,' he smiled. 'Let's get this testing done as soon as possible.' He took a sample of blood from Luna's arm and told them he'd be back in five minutes. True to his word, he arrived back in the room a few minutes later.

'It's good news. Congratulations!' he said, looking squarely at Will and Serena in the manner he had quite clearly learned to adopt in scenarios such as this. 'You're going to have a baby!'

Luna jumped up immediately and hugged them both. 'I can't believe it's bloody worked!' she said, her eyes bright with unshed tears.

29.
SEPTEMBER 2015

'I've got to go now,' Serena said.

'Hey, please, Serena. Don't let me scare you off. Please let's chat. We've got so much to catch up on.'

'We don't actually, Freddie. We aren't a part of each other's lives any more. We could have been. But you ended that. Please don't call me again.'

'If that's what you want . . .'

'It is . . . And Freddie,' she said.

'Yes?'

'If it had been anyone but her, I'd have forgiven you at the time.'

She hung up and drained the rest of her brandy.

On the short walk back to the Vicarage, Serena realised she felt revitalised. Perhaps the shock of hearing from Freddie had been a wake-up call, making her realise it was time to get things into perspective. Her life was here, right now, with Will, and it was important to make it work. As Will had so rightly told her, it was time to move on. Not to give up, as far as she was concerned, but definitely time to get on with life.

She arrived home and found Will in the study.

'I'm sorry,' she said, dashing over and sitting on his lap, running her hands through his thick red hair. 'I know I've not been helping by fixating on Mrs Pipe's curse. I'm going to tell the Colonel not to worry about doing the research. We need more than ever to work together to get the village on side and I promise I'm going to plough my energy into that, Will. Tomorrow I'm going to start organising the Harvest Supper and it's going to be the best damned party the village has ever known,' she gabbled.

Will laughed, clearly relieved, and hugged her to him. 'You're back,' he said and they kissed. Moments later, Will drew apart from Serena.

'I'm sorry too,' he said. 'Not just for offloading to Alice, but for getting cross at lunch. The stupid thing is, I keep telling you we need to move on, but I'm trying to convince myself just as much as you. I don't know what else to do . . .' Will hung his head, a gesture so unlike his usual optimistic and enthusiastic self that Serena felt incredibly protective of him.

'You're right, in many ways. We do need to move on. But, Will, please let's never give up hope. Hope is all there is.'

Will looked up. 'You're right. I promise. Let's allow ourselves that . . . hope,' he mumbled into Serena's ear and they hugged again, clinging to one another as though holding on for dear life.

❦

As promised, the next morning Serena began preparations for the Harvest Supper, which was only a month away. For this she needed, first and foremost, Alice.

'Are you free today?' she asked, calling at nine o'clock on the dot.

'Absolutely. Just back from dropping the children at school and I'm free until pickup. Shall I come to you?'

'Please. We need to get our thinking caps on.'

'Be with you in ten minutes.'

Serena made her way down to the kitchen and put the kettle on to boil, then rifled around in the larder and found the gluten-free brownies she'd made a couple of days ago in a burst of domesticity. She located teacups, teapot, milk jug and sugar bowl in the pantry and even found a starched white tablecloth, which she shook out and laid over the kitchen table. She returned to the pantry and picked out a couple of plates to match the tea set. It was an ancient set passed down from her maternal grandmother – fine white china with a pale pink-and-gold pattern. By the time Alice arrived, letting herself in, the kettle was boiling.

'Well, look at this, a tea party fit for a queen!' laughed Alice, as she settled herself down on one of the pine chairs.

'This is me showing I mean business,' Serena told her, filling the teapot with hot water and carrying it over to the beautifully laid table. 'I'll just let that stew a moment or two,' she said. 'And look – I've got a notepad and pen here too, to jot down all your good ideas.'

'Very organised. Now, let me get my diary out,' said Alice, reaching for a smooth leather book in her handbag. 'So, first things first: remind me of the date.'

'Friday the 23rd of October. I thought eight o'clock?'

'Let me write it in,' said Alice, scribbling away. 'You know, we don't actually have that long to get this organised. But sometimes that's a good thing – concentrates the mind. So . . . let's note down a few headings and then we'll deal with detail. "Venue and Furniture", "Food", "Drink", "Paid Help", "Music", "Decorations",

"Advertising", "Tickets" . . . Do you still want to go with Max's idea and make it cheap and rustic?'

'Yes, I think so,' said Serena. 'It's a massive risk, as I know it's always been so popular as a smarter do, but I just don't think we'll sell enough tickets . . .'

'You're right. Much better to make it free – far more likely to get lots of people coming along. But I think you'll need to make it ticketed anyway, even if they're free, so you can limit numbers to a manageable amount. I'll be in charge of making them and I'll draw up some posters too. I'll get all that done by the end of the week. I'll speak to Bob the butcher and Gill at the florist's and ask them to be in charge of giving away the tickets to anyone who's interested. You know, the Harvest Supper was always lovely, but it was a bit *stiff*. I think this will be much more like a Harvest Supper should be. Like something from a Hardy novel.'

'I do hope so,' Serena replied. 'We'll have it in the church hall, obviously, and we can use all the tables and chairs there, as well as all the crockery and cutlery. Glasses we'll need to hire, but that shouldn't be too expensive. Ashna has kindly said she'll make table-cloths – a different colour for every table – and we'll need some sort of centrepiece for each table: perhaps a cream church candle with ivy swathed around it?'

'I'm happy to make them. I've got a stack of candles. And Rob has a cellar absolutely full of wine. I'll get him to contribute a dozen bottles of his best Claret.'

'Really?'

'He's in no position to argue,' Alice answered crisply and Serena felt a teeny bit sorry for Rob, but was extremely grateful nonetheless.

'That would be fantastic. At least that way, we'll have a really good bottle on each table to start with. And perhaps we could say "bring your own" on the tickets too. If everyone brought one, we'd have masses. And Will's been busy brewing some of his own beer lately so we can offer that too.'

'What about decorations?' Alice wondered. 'You said Max thought it might be an idea to hang dried hops up all over the show . . .'

'Yes, a brilliant idea, don't you think? Shall I ask Jake?'

'Perfect, he's bound to be able to help – just the season for hop-picking and they'll make the hall smell divine. Now, food . . . Were you thinking lasagne, that kind of thing?'

'Yes, I'm going to make masses of lasagne, a gluten-free one too, a vegetarian dish and chilli con carne with rice and I'll freeze them all so we can just defrost them on the day. Then all we need to buy is some bread and salad to serve with them.'

'I'll get the bread, if you do the salad,' said Alice. 'And if it's a buffet, we won't need anyone to dish up; everyone can just help themselves one table at a time. You and I can heat everything up in the ovens in the hall kitchen – thank goodness they're those massive industrial ones – then bring it all out. I'm sure Ashna, Max and Pete would lend a hand too. We could maybe just ask Mrs Pipe to help with washing up afterwards? Puddings too, we need to think about. Now . . . one last thing. Music. No string quartet this year?'

'Nope. I'm going to get the piano in the church hall tuned next week and Will and I are going to practise a few hymns, so after the meal we'll hopefully get everyone joining in with some good old favourites – you know, "Jerusalem" and the like. "*And did those feet in ancient time . . .*"' Serena sang with gusto and Alice laughed.

Provisional plans made, they sat back and enjoyed their tea and brownies. After waving Alice off, Serena realised she hadn't thought about the curse all morning. This was definitely the turning point for her. And it was about time too.

30.
APRIL–JUNE 2014

Serena held back Luna's hair for about the thirtieth time that day, as she was sick into the loo. Serena's knees ached from being in this position all day so she could hardly bear to imagine how her poor sister must feel.

'This can't be normal,' Luna said eventually. Serena passed her a glass of water. Luna looked deathly pale. She was now eight weeks pregnant and this was her second week of being violently sick all day long. 'Why do they call it morning sickness? It's bloody all-day-long sickness. Serena, I can't handle much more of this. When will it stop?'

'I don't know. I'm so sorry,' Serena said, feeling guilty that Luna was going through all of this just for her. 'I think we should see a doctor. It doesn't seem right. I hope it doesn't indicate a problem with the baby.'

'Ring the doctor now,' Luna said as she groaned, her head dipping back into the loo. 'See if you can get an appointment today.'

Serena managed to and half an hour later they were sitting opposite Luna's GP.

'You're suffering with hyperemesis gravidarum, I'm afraid – a very rare condition that affects pregnant women. If it makes you feel any better, you're in good company. The Duchess of Cambridge suffers with it.'

'It doesn't!' Luna told him bluntly. She looked a wreck. Thin as a rake, her skin grey, her hair lank.

'How long have you been sick for?'

'Two weeks to the day,' Luna told him. 'Please tell me it's going to stop. I can't even go to work. I've had to take some unpaid leave. Serena has too,' she explained.

'I'm afraid it can last for weeks. Are you managing to eat and drink anything?'

'Yes, but it all comes up again about five minutes later. I'm being sick about forty times a day . . .' Luna stopped. She seemed to pale even more. 'Shit, everything's gone black,' she said, and a moment later she collapsed.

'Don't panic,' the doctor said to Serena. 'This can happen with her condition. She'll be fine, and so will the baby. But we need to get her to hospital. They'll put her on a drip and make sure the problem is managed now. Can you get the receptionist to call an ambulance?' he asked Serena, as he knelt down and gently moved Luna into the recovery position.

⁓

'How are you feeling?' Serena asked. It was evening now and Luna was in a ward, supine on a hospital bed and hooked up to a drip.

'So much better,' Luna told her, smiling weakly. 'But I can hardly stay in here for the rest of my pregnancy. What's going to happen?'

'I've spoken to a doctor,' Serena told her. 'Basically, the choice is ours. There are some anti-sickness drugs you can take that pose a very small risk to the baby, but will help you to carry on as normally as possible and actually allow you to get all the nutrients you and the baby need. Or you can carry on vomiting, passing out and being in and out of hospital to be put on a drip.'

'What a lovely choice,' Luna said, raising her eyebrows. 'I think it had better be your call.'

'Well, I've spoken to Will and we've agreed there's potentially more risk to the baby if you don't take the drugs, and it's just not fair on you to continue feeling so dreadful. We're happy for you to take the medication.'

'Are you sure?' Luna asked. 'Because I'll understand if you don't want me to.'

'We're sure,' Serena told her, squeezing her hand. 'Would you like some now?'

'Please,' Luna whispered, as she reached for a kidney-shaped bowl.

By the end of the next day, Luna had been able to return home and, as a result of the medication, the pregnancy continued much more smoothly.

*

It was now summer and the day of the eagerly anticipated twelve-week scan. Will and Serena met Luna at the hospital, nervously excited – increasingly so, as they were kept waiting an hour. Eventually, though, it was time.

'Baby's due on Christmas Eve, I see,' the sonographer said, and Will and Serena nodded: they could barely wait for their Christmas present.

'This will feel a bit cold,' the sonographer told Luna, as she rubbed cool jelly onto her stomach. Will and Serena gripped hands and the next thing they knew, they could see their baby on the screen. Everyone held their breath while various tests were conducted and measurements taken.

'Is everything okay?' Serena asked eventually. She noticed Luna was gazing at her navel, having clearly decided not to look at the picture of the baby. Zara had advised her to keep as detached as possible.

'Baby seems fine,' the lady told her with a smile. 'Look, it's waving at you!' she laughed. Will and Serena smiled.

'Are you okay?' Serena asked Luna. She was conscious that she and Will were so fixated on the baby it could be easy to overlook how Luna was feeling. She hoped her sister didn't feel too much like a vessel, rather than a human being.

'Of course,' she told them. 'But I'm dying for a wee. How much longer?' she asked.

'Nearly done,' the sonographer told her. 'And you won't need a full bladder for the next scan at twenty weeks, so that's something.'

'Thank heavens for that,' Luna replied.

'Can you tell the sex yet?' Will asked.

'Not yet. We'll probably be able to next time though, if you'd like to find out.'

Will and Serena looked at each other and nodded.

'Yes, definitely,' Will said.

'See you in a couple of months then,' the sonographer told them and, as Luna dashed off to the loo, Will and Serena stood in the corridor, wide-eyed with excitement.

'It's really happening,' Will said, wiping a tear away. 'A baby. Our baby. At last.'

31.
OCTOBER 2015

It was early October and Ashna stood nervously in the entrance hall, waiting for Will, wearing a black suit of Serena's (a relic from her working days).

'All set?' he asked.

'Ready as I'll ever be,' she replied.

'Good luck!' Serena told her, squeezing her tight. 'And remember, it's them on trial. Not you. Just answer the questions slowly and truthfully, and it will all be over before you know it. I'm going to spend the afternoon cooking for the Harvest Supper and I'll keep some of it for us to have for dinner. And I'll put some bubbly in the fridge. We can celebrate.'

'Let's just hope there's something *to* celebrate,' said Ashna, her dark eyes wide with fear.

'Think positively, Ashna. You're so good at that.'

Serena kissed Will and waved them off at the front door. She went back inside. The house felt very still and quiet with just her there. Max and Pete were also witnesses at the trial of Ashna's father and brother and had been advised to travel to Court separately.

Alice was due to arrive in the afternoon to help Serena with her batch cooking, but for now Serena was alone. It actually felt quite nice. She loved company, but sometimes she relished moments to herself. It felt like the ultimate luxury to be able to choose exactly what to do with her time for a few hours. Such luxury was curtailed very quickly. She'd just made herself a cup of tea and was contentedly fussing over Paddington by the Rayburn when she heard the doorbell.

'Morning!' It was the Colonel. 'Just on my way to the library to begin my research on the house,' he explained. 'Going to catch the bus into Rye, but it's not due for another half an hour. Thought I'd pop by, keep you briefed.'

'Come in!' welcomed Serena. 'Come and have a quick coffee before you get your bus.'

The Colonel followed Serena. With his solitary arm, his lanky frame and slightly skewed spectacles, there was something touchingly vulnerable about the Colonel, despite his rather military conversation style.

'Actually, I *wanted* to talk to you about the research. It's so kind of you to do it . . .' Serena began, about to tell him she no longer needed his help, having decided to take a no-nonsense approach to the matter. She flicked the kettle on, while the Colonel folded his long legs under the pine table.

'Doing me a favour, actually,' admitted the Colonel. 'Been a bit blue since Mrs Feltham-Jones passed, I must say. Dear Margo. Bit lonely, all things considered. Nice to feel useful at last. Thank you.' He accepted the mug of coffee Serena gave him. There was a slight tremor to his hand. Serena realised there was no way she could stand him down on the research. And what harm could it do? She would remain cool and level-headed now, whatever the result.

'I really appreciate it,' she said, joining the Colonel at the table. 'Now, tell me, will you be coming to the Harvest Supper?'

'Certainly will. Jake rang me last night. He's bagged me a ticket from the florist's. Going to pick me up and drive me home, save me a taxi fare.'

'That's kind of him. He's a good friend of yours, isn't he? How long have you known each other?'

'Used to be pals with his father, Bert. He used to run the farm, passed away a few years ago. Jake didn't deal with his death very well. His pa was all he had – mother ran off when he was three. Hit the whisky bottle, Jake did. My wife and I could see what was happening. We'd been through it with Margo, you see.'

'She was an alcoholic?'

'No, but an addict. Painkillers. She hurt her back, got hooked on the pain relief. An opiate addict. We got her sorted out in the end, and she became a counsellor – helping others in the same boat. So she saw the mess Jake had got himself into and helped him get back on the straight and narrow. He became like a son to us. Then Margo died, of course, which was hard for us both. Look after each other now, we do. Me and Jake.'

'You know he's left Tanya then? Moved into that B & B down the road?'

'Yes, writing was on the wall there with Tanya. Don't know why he's the one who's moved out.'

'I think it's only temporary, until she finds somewhere . . . Had you thought . . . It's only a suggestion, but what about if Jake moved in with you for a little bit?' suggested Serena, who then wished she hadn't. There was matchmaking, her speciality (until recently), and then there was interfering.

But, 'What a splendid idea!' said the Colonel, his face alight and animated. 'Why didn't I think of that? We could be company for each other. Do you know, just as soon as I get back from Rye I shall drop round and see him. Thank you, my dear. Now, I'd best be off. Don't want to miss the bus. I'll let you know just as soon as I've completed the research.'

Serena accompanied the Colonel up to the front door and stood, waving him off.

ॐ

Alice arrived at two o'clock, by which time the kitchen was strewn with pans, the scent of sizzling onions pervading the room.

'Why use one pan when you can use ten?' laughed Alice, taking in the mess.

'I know, I know,' giggled Serena. 'I'm so hopeless. Will usually does all the cooking and now I remember why!' She had red cheeks and her wild hair was even wilder than usual.

Alice rolled up her sleeves. 'Shall I take over the cooking or make a start on the clearing up?' she asked, finding an apron and popping it on. Serena noticed Alice definitely looked more relaxed. Still immaculate really, but now without her usual bright red nails, and with a more relaxed hairstyle. Even her stiff handbag had been replaced with a more slouchy leather number.

'I'm almost there now with the first batch,' said Serena. 'So could you make a start on the pans? Sorry!' She grimaced. 'This is when I wish I had a dishwasher.'

'No probs,' said Alice. 'That's why I'm here. Now, let me update you on what I've done since we last spoke. I made the tickets and delivered half to Bob the butcher and half to Gill at the florist's – sixty each, as I think the limit has to be a hundred and twenty . . .'

'We'll be lucky . . .' Serena interrupted.

'You never know. Let's be optimistic and plan for the best-case scenario. So, that's done. I've made the table centrepieces. Spoken to Rob and he's going to provide two cases of wine. Nice stuff too.'

'Two? But that's twenty-four bottles!'

'Told you; he'll do anything to please me at the moment,' Alice said with a wry smile, as she looked up from scouring a burnt pan. 'I must try not to enjoy the power too much,' she giggled, sounding so much more carefree than before. 'How about you?' she asked. 'Aside from this veritable feast you're cooking up today . . .'

'Ashna's finished all the tablecloths so they're ready. I've got two barrels of Will's homemade brew, which will probably have everybody legless. I've hired glasses from an off-licence in Rye. The rest is going to be a case of knuckling down on the day – setting up the tables, transporting the food, getting it all looking pretty. Max, Pete and Ashna are going to help. Oh, and Jake, of course. He's delivering masses of dried hops the day before, so Will and the boys are going to hang those all over the hall. I think the hops will make all the difference.'

'They will. The place will look and smell divine. And did you get the hall piano tuned?' Alice asked. She wasn't leaving anything to chance.

'Yep. Will and I have been practising in the evenings. We've been having such a laugh. Neither of us had played properly for ages so we were like Les Dawson to begin with.'

'Talking of which, I saw Gill at the florist's this morning. She said Miss Dawson has got herself a ticket so the village party animal will be there.'

'Let's hope it's not just us lot and her.'

'Ha! She'll be ticking you off for causing a nuisance if you play the piano past nine o'clock,' Alice chuckled.

'Do you know what?' asked Serena suddenly, yanking off her oven gloves. The lasagnes looked perfect – just a hint of the overcooked about them, which would give the topping a delicious crunch.

'What?' asked Alice.

'I'm actually looking forward to it. The Harvest Supper. It's something I was dreading. And thanks to you, I'm excited about it now. Thank you so much.'

But Alice wasn't one for soppiness. 'Nothing to do with me,' she said rather briskly, but then softened and added, 'But thanks anyway.'

❦

By seven o'clock that evening, two batches of food had been prepared and the kitchen was pristine. Serena was exhausted but satisfied. There was no sign of Will and Ashna or the boys so she turned off the kitchen lights, leaving just a couple of lamps burning on the dresser, and made her way upstairs to the bedroom. There she turned on more lamps, stoked the fire she'd lit earlier and pulled the pale blue curtains firmly closed. She looked at the bed and saw that Paddington was snuggled into her pillow. She stroked her briefly then padded through to the en suite, where she turned on the taps, filling the enormous Victorian bath with hot water and bubble bath. The whole room smelled immediately of pine essence. Serena undressed, hopped into the bath and lay back, letting her long curls meander in the water like Medusa's snakes. There was, she decided, nothing quite like a hot scented bath after an afternoon spent cooking and scouring pans.

As she lay in the steaming water, she thought about Ashna and hoped she hadn't had too much of a traumatic day. She'd received a text from Will to say Ashna's father and brother had pleaded guilty at the last minute, so at least the poor girl hadn't had to give evidence in the end.

Then she closed her eyes, her mind wandering. And suddenly she found her thoughts drifting into dangerous territory. It was October. More than a year since it had all happened. She remembered the day so well. The brasserie, the flat, the fridge . . .

Before her thoughts could descend into the well-worn pattern of dark despair they tended to follow once sparked, she heard a car. They were back. She jumped out of the bath, dried herself and chucked some clothes on.

'And?' she said, bounding down the stairs in her jeans and a navy jumper, wet hair bouncing around her shoulders. She paused halfway down. Ashna and the boys stood in the hallway, shedding themselves of coats and jackets.

'Two years!' Ashna shouted up, clearly delighted. 'They didn't get much for the affray or the assault, but the judge was keen to make an example of them under the new law on forced marriages. They both got two years! I feel like I can breathe again. I don't have to keep looking over my shoulder. For a little while anyway.'

'They're not going to be bothering you again,' said Max protectively, and he pulled Ashna towards him.

'This calls for champagne!' said Serena, racing down the last of the stairs and hugging them all, happy to be distracted again.

32.
AUGUST–SEPTEMBER 2014

'Are you nearly here?' Luna asked impatiently. 'I'm the next one in.'

'It's the bloody traffic. We're completely stuck. Are you not delayed? Last time we had to wait an hour.' Serena had her mobile clamped to her ear, her other hand running through her hair in exasperation as Will sat at the wheel. They were static and at least half an hour away from the hospital. It was also baking hot and, with no air con in the car, they both had sweat running uncomfortably down their backs.

'No, they're running on time today. What should I do? Ask for a later appointment?'

'No, don't do that. They might put you off and we want to find out today. Just make sure the baby's okay and don't forget to ask about the sex!'

'I will, don't worry. Just try to get here.'

'We'll do everything we can. Good luck!'

'Thanks . . .'

Half an hour later, Will and Serena raced into the antenatal department. They found Luna in the waiting room.

'Are we too late?' Serena asked, dashing over.

'Afraid so, but don't worry – it was all perfect. The sonographer said the baby is fine and dandy. I didn't look at the screen or these pictures, but here they are.' Luna handed over an envelope. Will immediately opened it and he and Serena gazed lovingly at the black-and-white blobs, trying to work out which body part was which.

'Look, there's its hand,' said Serena.

'No, that's a foot,' Will said, head on one side, trying to work it out.

'You can stop calling the baby 'it' now,' Luna told them, rubbing her belly. 'We're cooking up a boy in here. A baby boy!' She grinned and the three of them hugged.

'I can't believe it's a boy!' Serena laughed. 'I don't know why, but I was convinced it was a girl. I need to look at boys' names now.'

'Didn't we think Cuthbert would be nice for a boy?' Will asked innocently. Serena and Luna both thumped him on the arm.

'What shall we do now?' Luna asked. 'I've got the whole afternoon off work.'

'Let's go shopping!' Serena said, her eyes bright. 'Let's go shopping for blue!'

'Count me out,' said Will. 'But I'll come into town with you and find a nice shady pub garden somewhere to read the paper. Come and find me when you two are done. And please don't spend too much . . .' he said, without much hope.

They were off, like a couple of excited schoolgirls.

Two weeks later and it was the start of September, one of Serena's favourite times of year. She loved the misty mornings that blossomed into sunny days then cooled into dusky evenings. The feeling of return-to-school that made her want to buy a brand-new pencil case and start an exercise book afresh.

It was a Saturday and they were due to meet Luna for brunch at their favourite brasserie just down the road. They arrived first and dithered over whether to sit inside or out. The breeze was a little cool but the sun was warming up. They plumped for a table on the pavement where they could people-watch as well as chat among themselves. The relationship between the three of them was cosy and comfortable these days, and Luna usually had them in stitches as she commented mercilessly on other diners or passers-by.

'Table opposite, eating irons negative,' she would say, out of the corner of her mouth, ridiculing the poor unsuspecting soul who'd never learnt to hold his knife and fork correctly. 'And why, do tell me, did that woman think it appropriate to leave the house wearing her granny's curtains? Poor thing. Clearly doesn't own a mirror.' Will and Serena would feel guilty and try not to laugh, but it was almost impossible.

'What can I get you?' asked the waiter, finding them seated and perusing the menus.

'Freshly squeezed orange juice, please,' said Serena.

'Bloody Mary for me,' Will ordered. 'Should we get something for Luna? She likes sparkling elderflower, doesn't she?'

'Yes, one of those, please. And we'll have food too, but we'll just wait for my sister to arrive.'

'Okay, no probs,' said the waiter, pocketing his notepad and disappearing inside.

Will spread out his weekend papers and Serena checked her phone.

'We did say eleven, didn't we?' she asked. It was half past now.

'You know what she's like, Serena. Never on time. We're in no rush.'

'True,' she agreed, and sifted through Will's paper, finding the property supplement. She loved fantasising about living in a huge great mansion. She began reading.

'Ready to order yet?' The waiter was back. It was a quarter to twelve.

'Do you think she's okay?' Serena asked Will.

'I'm sure she is. She's probably forgotten. Baby brain. Tell you what, you stay here and I'll nip round the corner to her flat and see where's she's got to.'

'Okay, be quick,' said Serena. 'Sorry,' she said, turning to the waiter. 'We should be ready to order as soon as my sister gets here.'

'Just give me a shout,' he said. Serena watched Will disappear round the corner. She twirled her curls around her finger. She seriously hoped Luna was okay. And not just her, of course. The baby too.

Five minutes later, Will was back.

'No answer,' he said. 'She must have gone out somewhere. Obviously totally forgotten about our arrangement. Let's eat and then we'll try again on our way home.'

'Okay,' agreed Serena, but she started to feel the stirrings of worry. She batted them away and ordered her bacon and eggs.

ᘓᘔ

An hour later, they'd finished brunch and the sun's rays were much stronger. Serena fished around in her bag then put on her sunglasses. She checked her watch again.

'Will, I've got a funny feeling about this. Let's nip back and get the spare key from ours. Imagine if she's slipped over in the bath or something awful.'

By now, Will was starting to worry too, and they hurried back home, grabbed the spare key and were back at Luna's flat within minutes, in through the communal door and up in the lift to the top floor. Serena opened the door to the apartment.

It was tidy. Fastidiously so. And Luna was not a tidy person. They peered around.

'Luna?' Serena called out. No answer. They checked each room, but the flat was deadly silent. Serena went to Luna's bed and looked underneath, where she knew she kept her suitcase.

'Will, her case has gone,' Serena shouted out, her voice panicky. 'Quick, check her desk: third drawer down. That's where she keeps her passport.'

'Are you sure?' Will asked, rifling around. 'There's nothing in here . . . Ah, here it is,' he said, breathing a sigh of relief. Serena took it from him.

'Out of date,' she said. 'Look!'

'Well, maybe she just fancied a holiday,' Will said, casting around for an explanation for this sudden and unexpected departure. 'I mean, just because she's carrying our baby, she doesn't have to tell us everything . . .'

'Will, don't you think she might have mentioned it? I mean, if it was just an innocent break? Let me check the kitchen again.'

Serena dashed back through the hall, scanning the room for clues. She opened the fridge. It was spotless and empty. Not so much as a pint of milk. She realised there was no hum and the interior was dark. She shut the door, glancing at the various postcards stuck to it with fridge magnets. She closed her eyes. Then opened them again.

'Will!' she called. In seconds he was beside her. 'Look!' she said. And there, among the cards, was a note.

'*I'm sorry.*'

She was gone.

PART THREE

33.
OCTOBER 2015

'What do you think?' asked Serena, stepping to the back of the church hall to survey the sight in front of them. There were twelve trestle tables in a semicircle, each set up with ten chairs and covered in beautiful, vibrant tablecloths – each one a different colour so the whole display looked like a rainbow. Crockery, cutlery, glasses and napkins had been laid out and Alice's delightful candle and ivy centrepieces had been placed in the middle of each table, ready to be lit as darkness fell. Serving tables covered in starched white cloths had been situated next to the kitchen – salads and baskets of bread were on one, all neatly cling-filmed – and on the other there was plenty of space for all the hot food that would be brought out later. Homemade puddings were in the fridge too – trifles and tiramisus and a massive crumble (Will, Ashna and Alice had prepared these between them).

The best decorations of all though, were the dried hops that hung from the hall ceiling; as well as looking gloriously rustic, they gave a warm and drunken smell to the place. To add a further touch, Jake had provided a few bales of hay, which were stacked up in several areas ready to be sat on or leaped over as desired. Finally, to give even more of a sense of harvest, Serena had filled two large wooden baskets with freshly dug vegetables from the garden.

Alice stood back and looked all around her. 'Amazing,' she said. 'Even if I do say so myself. And it was a great idea to put all the heaters on yesterday. It feels warm and snug for a change. Oh, Serena, it looks great, doesn't it? And I like how you've pulled the piano into the room more, and with space around so people can come and join in if they want to.'

'That's what we thought. Alice, I'm so nervous now. What if no one turns up. All this work . . .'

'Well, most of the tickets have gone according to Bob and Gill, so it's a question of whether anyone actually gets off their bottom and turns up. All we can do is keep our fingers crossed. But look, it's gone five now. Time we headed home and dolled ourselves up. Have a little sherry or something for Dutch courage, and I'll see you back here at seven thirty.'

'Okay, see you later,' Serena replied, straightening one last piece of cutlery before turning out all the lights and vanishing along the lane towards the Vicarage. The cool air smelled of damp twigs, leaf litter and smoky bonfires. Serena inhaled it deeply: autumn was well and truly here.

The house had a feeling of anticipation to it, decided Serena, as she let herself in. From the hallway she could hear the sound of a bath running upstairs and jazz music drifting up from the kitchen. She bumped into Max, who was dashing through the hall with a small tray of drinks in his hands – two bottles of beer and a glass of wine.

'Has the party started already?' Serena asked with a smile.

'Thought it would be rude not to,' answered Max with a cheerful grin. 'Ashna has ordered a glass of Chardonnay to drink in the bath – very decadent – and Pete and I are having a little drink and card game before we start getting ready. Will's down in the kitchen. What time do we need to leave?'

'Seven twenty-five,' Serena told him precisely. 'That'll give us half an hour to hover around anxiously, wondering if anyone will turn up.'

'That gives us loads of time,' said Max. 'It's not even six yet,' he said and Serena smiled. Typical man. She wasn't one to spend hours getting ready, but even she knew it was about time she headed upstairs to wash her hair.

The hall was packed, every single seat taken, and a pleasant, light-hearted hum of chatter and laughter filled the room. Faces were red and cheerful, even Miss Dawson's (the Colonel and Jake Hardy had drawn the short straw and were gallantly sitting on either side of her, the Colonel with a generous hand for Miss Dawson's wine glass), and the carefully laid tables were now strewn with scraped-clean pudding bowls and dirty napkins, as well as half-filled glasses. The parishioners were taking full advantage of the food and drink on offer.

At half past ten, Will tapped on a glass and eventually, after a couple of false starts, he began a brief speech.

'Ladies and gents . . . Firstly, may I thank you with all my heart for turning up tonight. It means the world to Serena and me. It's been a funny old start to life in the village. I really mucked up by forgetting Fay Holland's wedding and then there was the prang at the crem – understandably there's been a bit of bad feeling from some quarters since then. Unfortunately, I am horribly human. But I want to tell you all that we love it here in Cattlebridge, and we don't want to leave. All I ask is that you give us a chance . . . A chance to make it work,' he said, a slight break in his voice.

'If I may . . .' said Bob the butcher, standing up. Will nodded. 'I personally think you're both a breath of fresh air and I'm sure I'm not alone in thinking this has been the best Harvest Supper we've known here in the village . . . And it's not over yet. In my humble opinion, you've done a brilliant job.'

'Hear, hear!' shouted the Colonel, rising to his feet and starting to clap his one hand onto the table. The parishioners looked around and, one by one, they began to stand and clap and cheer – even the Huntingdon-Loxleys. Will and Serena smiled at each other. Relief. They had done it.

'Thank you!' Will said when the applause eventually died down. 'And one more thing. We've started a Youth Club and we don't yet have any members, so if you know any youngsters who may be interested, please just let me or Serena know . . .'

'I'll send an email round at the school!' piped up a very pretty, lively-looking young woman, who Will recognised as the headmistress of the local secondary.

'Perfect,' grinned Will. 'Now, without further ado, let's really get this party started. Serena, what's the opening number?' he asked, turning to the piano.

'"Jerusalem"!' she shouted out, perched on the piano stool, and began to belt it out, the crowd soon joining in, Max and Pete banging on tables with gusto as they competed to sing the loudest.

And did those feet in ancient time
Walk upon England's mountains green?
And was the holy Lamb of God
On England's pleasant pastures seen?

And did the Countenance Divine
Shine forth upon our clouded hills?
And was Jerusalem builded here,
Among those dark Satanic Mills?

Bring me my Bow of burning gold!
Bring me my Arrows of desire!
Bring me my Spear: O clouds unfold!
Bring me my Chariot of fire!

I will not cease from Mental Fight,
Nor shall my sword sleep in my hand,
Till we have built Jerusalem
In England's green and pleasant land.

The applause as Serena finished was deafening and all of a sudden people were shouting out requests. 'Guide Me, O Thou Great Redeemer' seemed to be a hot favourite, so she struck up the introductory chords and another bellowing rendition began.

Then Will took over and soon the requests changed from hymns to pop classics and Serena found herself being swung around the room by Pete to Van Morrison's 'Brown Eyed Girl' and an old favourite – 'All Around My Hat' from Steeleye Span. Everyone, even Miss Dawson, seemed to be up from the tables and jigging around the piano, crashing into each other and tripping over the hay bales to gales of laughter. Serena noticed that the Smythes seemed like rather good fun, which came as a surprise. Mrs Pipe had not painted a kind picture of them.

After several upbeat numbers, including a raucous sing-along to 'Delilah' and Squeeze's 'Cool for Cats', the tempo changed and Will began to play Billy Joel's 'She's Always a Woman to Me'. Although perhaps the lyrics were more suited to a person like Luna than Serena, somehow it had once become 'their' song and, as Will sang, Serena sat down next to him on the piano stool and together they played a duet. Max and Ashna swayed together, a stunning couple with their dark, striking looks. Rob, meanwhile, reached out tentatively for Alice's hand. She took it.

Finally, it was midnight and time for the party to end.

'One more tune!' sang out Miss Dawson, and Serena and Alice exchanged amused glances.

'Oh, go on then!' said Will and he began to play John Denver's old classic, 'Take Me Home, Country Roads' – appropriate, he thought, as a finale.

By the time they got home, it was one o'clock in the morning and everyone was in high spirits and not remotely tired. Serena noticed an unfamiliar car parked outside the house and, as she tried to peer inside, the passenger door suddenly opened.

'Oh, thank goodness you're back!' said Stephanie, as she came towards Serena and embraced her in the sort of hug she'd rarely dished out in her life.

'Mum?' Serena said, taken aback. 'What are you doing here?'

'I've brought you a present,' she said, opening the rear passenger door and, after some fumbling, lifting out a little person, bundled up in an all-in-one. A teeny little person, with a thumb in their mouth, all warm and sleepy. Serena took the baby from her mother and the child clung to her like a little koala.

'Your baby,' smiled Stephanie, and Serena burst into tears.

34.
OCTOBER 2015

Serena was crying and smiling like a maniac, all at the same time. Will came to her side to look at the baby in the glow of the streetlight.

'He's a pretty little thing, isn't he?' he said in wonder.

'Ah, well, that's because *he* is actually a *she*. Luna lied about the sex. You've got a little girl!' exclaimed Stephanie.

'What?' Will and Serena replied in unison, but Stephanie decided at this point that it was no good trying to explain everything out in the dark, in the middle of the night.

'Let's not hang around out here any longer,' she said.

'No, of course not,' said Will. 'Did you come on your own?'

'No, Sebastian's in the car,' she said. 'And Brian.'

'What, Seb? Luna's old boyfriend?' asked Serena. 'And who's Brian?'

'Let's all get inside,' said Stephanie, 'then I'll explain everything.'

Car doors were opened and slammed again, Ashna unlocked the front door and they all piled into the hall.

'Come into the study,' said Will. 'The log burner will still be lit, so it'll be nice and warm. I'm Will,' he said, shaking hands with

Brian and everyone began politely introducing themselves while Serena just stood and beamed at the little bundle in her arms.

'Why don't I go and get us all some drinks?' suggested Ashna and she, Max and Pete headed down to the kitchen while Will and Serena led everyone else through to the study. Stephanie had been for Sunday lunch a couple of times since they'd first moved in, but hadn't been over in a while and she complimented them on how refreshed the house was looking.

'Now,' said Stephanie, sitting on one of the sofas and dusting down her skirt. 'Let me start by explaining about Brian. He's my boyfriend,' she said, looking a little bashful, and she reached out a hand towards him, which he clasped. He was a benevolent-looking sort of chap. Short and round, with ruddy cheeks.

Serena was sitting on the sofa opposite Stephanie and Brian, Will beside her and the baby snuggling up, almost asleep now, while Seb stood with his back against the fireplace, eager to stretch out his legs after the long journey.

'Your boyfriend?'

'Yes, Serena. You mustn't repeat everything I say or we'll be here all night. With all the business that went on with you and Luna, I was feeling a bit out of sorts. You'd withdrawn into yourself and clearly didn't want to see anyone, and Luna had disappeared. So I decided to take up a new hobby. Salsa dancing. I met Brian and, well, things have moved quite quickly. I'm happy with Brian,' she admitted, her cheeks a little red. 'I've stopped being quite so fixated about how things *look*. But anyway, that's by the by. One evening, Brian and I had just got back from our dance class when I received a phone call from Seb.'

At this point Ashna, Max and Pete arrived in the room bearing two bottles of red wine and a number of glasses. Max started to pour and dish the glasses out.

'So this is your baby?' asked Ashna, astonished. 'You never said . . .'

'Yes,' Serena told her. 'We thought we'd lost her forever. Will and I didn't tell anyone what had happened to us before we came here. We were trying to make a fresh start. Mum was just about to tell me how they managed to track this darling girl down, but it might be best if I explain, in a nutshell, what happened first.'

'Oh, please do, if you can bear to wait,' said Ashna.

'I've waited this long,' said Serena, and she began.

'After years of trying for a baby with no luck, Luna – my twin – offered to be our surrogate. It was successful and we were so excited. Luna seemed totally on board with it all, although we should probably have been more cautious. I've always known she had a ruthless streak.

'Anyway, we weren't. One September day, Luna failed to turn up for brunch with us so we dropped round to her flat and found that she'd disappeared. Her suitcase and passport were missing and we found a note on the fridge. "*I'm sorry*," it said, just like that. No explanations. Nothing.

'We were devastated, but at first we were fairly confident we'd be able to track her down before the baby was born. She was six months pregnant so we had three months before the due date – Christmas Eve. We rushed to our local police station first of all. Explained everything to a sympathetic young WPC. She took statements from us both before explaining, as tactfully as she could, that there wasn't an awful lot they could do. Legally, the baby was Luna's. But she did say we could register Luna as a missing person. The police agreed to do what they could to assist in finding her, although the officer explained that, if they did find her, it would be up to Luna whether details of her whereabouts could be passed on. They searched her flat and asked me to provide a recent photo and details of friends and relatives. But it felt a little as though they were going through the motions to placate us and nothing came of any of it.

'We rang our lawyer, but he just confirmed the same sad truth – legally, nothing could be done, even if Luna could be traced. In the end, we hired a private investigator. Our parish were wonderful – they had a whip-round so that we could afford him – and he worked pretty tirelessly. But Luna had left nothing to chance. She'd shut down her Facebook account a month before she left, her email had been deactivated, her mobile left behind. She'd paid the rent on her flat until the end of November and asked her landlord to put her belongings into storage at that point, providing the money for this, but no contact details.

'I think one of the hardest things to come to terms with was that she'd planned it all. It hadn't been a spur-of-the-moment decision about which she might suddenly see sense, but a premeditated act of utter selfishness. We only hoped she hadn't planned it from the start.

'By Christmas – the baby's due date – it was clear Luna had completely disappeared. We couldn't afford to keep the investigator on, so we thanked him for his efforts and spent a miserable Christmas conducting our own detective work to no avail. She could have been anywhere in the world. I gave up work, unable to carry on in the state I was in, and in the new year Will saw the job in Cattlebridge advertised – they needed a vicar to start in February – and the London parish agreed to allow Will to leave swiftly given the circumstances. We decided the only thing we could possibly do was try to start again. I never gave up hope, but it was unhealthy trying to carry on in our old parish. Too many questions from sympathetic friends and parishioners. It would have been impossible to move on. So we did it. Or, rather, Will did it. I was hopeless, but I went along with it all and we ended up here. And then, of course, Mrs Pipe told me about the curse.'

'Oh, goodness, no wonder you were so worried,' said Ashna, her eyes full of sympathy.

'The curse?' asked Stephanie.

'That's a whole other story,' said Serena, looking at her mother. 'And I don't think I can wait any longer. Please,' she said, 'tell me what happened. Tell me how you found our baby.'

35.
OCTOBER 2015

'It all began with a phone call to Sebastian,' Stephanie said. 'Actually, perhaps you'd better start,' she continued, offering the conversational baton to Seb. He nodded and took a quick gulp of wine. Serena thought the poor chap looked wrung out, dark bags under his eyes and his hair a mess.

'I hadn't been in touch with Luna for years – not since I broke it off with her all those years ago. It was January. I'd split up with my girlfriend, Karen, just before Christmas and was feeling a bit sorry for myself. Then, out of the blue, I received a phone call from Luna. I have no idea how she'd found my number, but she had. She told me she'd been in a violent relationship and had run off when she was heavily pregnant. Said she hadn't been able to stay in touch with anyone, even her family, and was feeling really lonely. It was one of those moments, when two worlds collide and the timing feels right.

'*"Where are you?"*' I asked.

'She said, "*Do you promise you won't tell anyone, even my family if they ask you?*" and I assumed she was terrified about this bloke finding her.

'"*Of course*",' I said. '"*Anyway, I'm not even in touch with your family.*" So she said she was in Scotland, somewhere remote. She asked if I'd go and stay with her for a bit. So I booked a couple of weeks off work – I was feeling in need of a bit of adventure – and flew up to Inverness, then hired a car and drove up the A9 and off the beaten track, eventually finding the little bothy she was renting.

'When I got there, I could see why she wanted some company. Totally marooned in the middle of nowhere and with just the baby to chat to. She seemed to be coping alright though. It was all a bit messy and chaotic but, Serena, what I can assure you about is that she took care of the baby. She said she'd had a home birth, there in the bothy. Luna bottle-fed – she said she'd tried to breastfeed but found it too painful. And the baby looked well enough. A sweet little thing. She can only have been a few weeks old that first visit. It was all a bit of a funny situation but I suppose, inevitably, we got back together. It had to be long-distance though, so I would fly back and forth from Gatwick every couple of weeks. She refused to travel anywhere herself.

'I suppose it would have carried on like that for some time, but last weekend Luna began to behave a bit strangely. She was overly clingy when it was time for me to go. Said she was feeling depressed. Begged me to stay. I couldn't though. Had to get back to work. But I was worried about her so a couple of days later I flew back up. I hadn't told her. I just thought it was important to get there. I let myself in the back door and went straight through to the bedroom. The baby was fast asleep in her cot, but there was no sign of Luna. So I looked in the bathroom. And there she was, self-harming – cutting herself with a razor blade.'

There was an audible intake of breath in the room, and Serena's hand shot up to her mouth.

'She was horrified I'd discovered her and I was horrified I hadn't realised how seriously depressed she was. She implored me not to tell anyone. Said she didn't want any agencies to get involved, in case it led the ex-boyfriend back to her. So I promised I wouldn't tell anyone. Fortunately for you, I broke that promise.'

'Who did you tell?' asked Serena.

'Your mother.'

36.
OCTOBER 2015

'He rang me up. We'd just got back from dance class, hadn't we, Brian? He said, "*Stephanie, it's Sebastian. I need to talk to you about Luna.*"

'"*Luna?*" I asked, my heart pounding. "*Have you seen her?*"

'"*Yes,*" he told me. "*We're going out with each other again. She didn't want me to tell anyone, in case that thug of an ex-boyfriend tracked her down.*"

'"*What ex-boyfriend?*"

'"*The one who battered her. The one she escaped from. Listen, I think it's really affected her. She's depressed. She's started to self-harm. I'm worried about whether she can care for the baby,*" he said.

'"*Oh, my Lord,*" I said. Brian had to get me a chair so I could sit down. "*Seb,*" I said to him. "*The baby isn't hers.*" Poor Seb, another innocent victim in all of this. I explained everything to him, about the surrogacy and her disappearing. He told me where they were, gave me directions, and suggested I just get there and confront her. Better not to give her a chance to escape beforehand. So Brian and I left the following day – drove all the way. When we got there, Brian stayed in the car and I went in and we had the most almighty row.

'I was worried about the baby as she was crying. So I took her out to Brian and he cuddled her in the car. Luna was going mad and Seb had to restrain her, didn't you? Then she just dissolved into tears. Seb stayed with her, while I dashed about picking up whatever I thought the baby might need. We've got a cot for her – it's in the car. Then Luna ran into the bathroom and locked herself in. We knew what she was doing. It pains me to say it, but we called the mental health authorities.'

'What happened then?' asked Serena.

'She was sectioned.'

'And now?' Will asked.

'She's in a special unit, getting treatment in Inverness. I explained to her through the bathroom door that we were going to return the baby to her rightful parents. I think she knew, really, that it was inevitable. It's the genes, you know,' Stephanie said.

'What do you mean?' Serena asked, stroking the baby's cheek as she dozed on her shoulder.

'You know your father was a Barnardo's child? Well, he and his twin brother looked their mother up years later and it transpired she suffered with a personality disorder. They never met – Arthur didn't want to meet her. But it was clear she'd always been quite unstable. I look back now and realise how moody Luna was, even as a little girl. Moody and impulsive and quite ruthless. Do you remember Elizabeth?' Serena nodded, recalling the long-ago incident when her sister had stolen her doll.

'Mind you, I thought she'd improved. Think she just got better at hiding it, don't you?'

'Yes,' whispered Serena.

'How I wish I'd warned you against the surrogacy at the time. I was worried. I started to tell you it wasn't a good idea, but you didn't want to hear, and I'd learnt the hard way not to interfere in your lives when I'd told Seb about Freddie. I was in such trouble about that. Anyway, I suppose it's as well I didn't talk you out of it in the long run, or we wouldn't have this gorgeous baby here . . . But let's not dwell any longer. It's three o'clock in the morning. Time we all went to bed. We can carry on talking tomorrow,' Stephanie said, stifling a yawn.

'Good idea,' said Will. 'And we must find beds for you all. There are plenty. But just a couple more things,' he added. 'Stephanie, why did Luna tell us we were expecting a boy?'

'To make herself harder to trace, I'd have thought. You were looking for a woman with a baby boy, after all,' she replied.

'Of course . . . And Stephanie, what's her name? The baby? It seems a bit late in the day to change it.'

'She's called Winter,' smiled Stephanie. 'A Christmas baby, remember?'

'How could we ever forget?'

37.

OCTOBER–NOVEMBER 2015

The week that followed was full of excitement, disturbed sleep while Winter settled in, and a little sadness too.

'She's ten months old, Will. She'll be walking soon. I'm so unbelievably grateful to have her at all, but I can't help feeling a bit of grief for those precious lost months. And what about the legal side of things? We'll still need to get a parental order, won't we?'

'I'll contact our lawyer and find out what we need to do. Don't worry about it though, my darling. I'm sure it'll all be straightforward now.' He sighed. 'I know what you mean about the lost months though – I feel the same. But at least she's here. And healthy. And she's taken to you. Just look at her.' Winter was in Serena's arms, being fed her bottle, looking up at her true mother adoringly. It probably helped that Serena looked identical to the only mother Winter had known until now.

'Yes,' Serena said, smiling. 'And I was thinking, we must get her christened. When shall we do it?'

'I think we need to have a period of calm first, let everything settle down. Stephanie and Brian are leaving tomorrow, but we've invited them for Christmas so why don't we have the christening then? Maybe on Christmas Eve?'

'Perfect!' Serena agreed and Winter batted away the bottle, looked up at her mum and smiled, a little dimple in each cheek, her eyes a deep sapphire blue.

༄

It was early November and the household had settled into a new routine with Winter, who was a highly sociable and amusing little character. She laughed like a drain at the smallest of prompts, wrinkling her nose with amusement, and everyone in the house loved her, even Mrs Pipe.

'She favours her father,' she'd said on meeting her. 'Reverend Blacksmith through and through, this nipper, and right lusty she is too,' she'd added, remarking on her chubby cheeks.

Winter took the adoration in her stride and had taken a particular shine to Pete. One chilly November afternoon, he arrived in the kitchen to find Serena feeding Winter in the new high chair, while Will cooked supper.

'Hi, Pete,' said Will. 'Are you joining us for supper later?' He twisted pepper onto the marinated chicken in front of him on the central work table.

'Please. Actually, I've got some news,' he said, scraping back a chair and plonking himself down. 'I've got meself a job,' he told them, smiling proudly. 'You'd have thought it weren't possible for an ex-con to find a place to live or a decent job if you listened to the screws, but it turns out there are some proper nice people out there. You've both been too good to me, but it's all changed now for you. You're a family all of a sudden. Time for me to move on.'

'You know you'd be welcome to stay regardless,' said Serena. 'But it's fantastic news you've found a job. That's next on the agenda for me too. I'm going to train to be a midwife at long last. What are you going to be doing?' she asked, spooning yogurt into Winter's mouth. She was a good eater, if a bit of a messy one.

'Landscape gardener for a small set-up in South Devon. I had the interview through Skype and I 'fessed up to me past, but the geezer wasn't bothered. I'd already emailed him some plans and ideas, and those before and after photos of the Vicarage garden. That was enough for him. He's going to let me a cottage too.'

'Whereabouts in South Devon?' asked Will.

'Thatchley, the town's called. Never heard of it, but it's not too far from Totnes, he said.'

'Thatchley? I know it!' said Will. 'Some old friends of ours live in a little village nearby – Potter's Cove. We're inviting them to the christening, so I'll introduce you. You will still be here for it?'

'Wouldn't miss little Winnie's big day, would I, darlin'?' he asked, tickling Winter's feet. She giggled. 'I'll stay till just after Chrimbo, if that's alright? Job starts in the new year.'

'We'll miss you,' said Serena, getting up and giving him a kiss. 'But you're right. A fresh start for us all. A proper one this time. And, talking of which, I must get on. I'm meeting Alice at the pub to find out what's happening with her and Rob. Are you happy to take over?' she asked Will, offering him Winter's spoon, but Pete took it instead and pulled up a chair to finish the feeding fest.

38.
NOVEMBER 2015

Alice was already installed in a booth near the fire when Serena arrived. She jumped up and gave Serena a kiss, smelling as she always did – of Chanel No. 5, that timeless classic that suited her so well.

'I've got you a sherry,' she said to Serena. 'I remembered you saying it's your tipple at this time of year. Is that okay?' she asked.

'Perfect,' said Serena, taking a sip. 'Now, tell me. What on earth's going on? Are you seriously going back to Rob? Why the change of heart?'

'I know, I know . . . I totally see why it must seem crazy to you. We're going to give it another try. I probably look like a complete mug, but – as ever with these things – it's complicated.'

'I really like Rob, don't get me wrong,' Serena said, taking another warming sip of sherry. 'But I just hope he's learnt his lesson this time . . .'

'So do I, but I think finally leaving him was the best thing I ever did. Not just because it taught him a lesson and showed him I was serious, but because it's enabled me to go back to being me again. The "me" I was when we first fell in love with each other.'

'I must admit, you *do* seem to have changed quite a bit since you left him.'

'Not really changed,' Alice explained. 'Actually, probably just reverted slightly to the person Rob fell in love with.' She looked into her vodka and tonic and sighed.

'How did you meet?' asked Serena, realising she didn't know anything about their early days as a couple.

'I was in my thirties and working as an events planner in London. You'll probably find this hard to believe but I'm actually from a very working-class background. I got a scholarship to a boarding school in Kent for my sixth form and made friends with all the right people. Most of the Berrywood pupils went to university but some of us found jobs in London – doing things like events planning. My friend Suzie had all the right contacts and so my career began with her help. Every year we were tasked with planning the medics' ball for the doctors and nurses at St Thomas's. If you planned the damned thing, then you had to be there for it and this particular ball was always a total scream. Doctors and nurses are the naughtiest lot. I should have known then,' Alice said, smiling wryly at Serena.

'Anyway, I met Rob; we got together. I was a completely different person back then. Chubby, with wavy hair I didn't know what to do with: I *looked* like another person. And, thinking back, I *felt* like a different person too. Carefree. At ease. A *joie de vivre* that's sadly evaporated somewhat as the years have passed. But – and this is cringingly embarrassing to admit – I didn't even *sound* the same!'

'What do you mean?' asked Serena.

'I still had a pretty rough accent back then, despite my time at Berrywood. When I realised Rob and I were serious, I had elocution lessons.'

'But why?' asked Serena, amazed at the lengths Alice had gone to.

'It was the other doctors' wives and girlfriends – the WAGs. As soon as I met them, I realised I was another species. So my campaign began to stamp out as much of the real Alice as I possibly could. Now, I'm not saying that Rob has been justified in having all these affairs, but what I can admit is that Rob married the person he fell in love with, and that person was quickly usurped by a much classier individual. And the trouble is, of course, that trying so hard to be someone you're not makes you tense, anxious, a perfectionist. I transformed myself beautifully. But, looking back, I was a victim of my own success.'

'So what happened to make you realise all this?' asked Serena.

'It was leaving Rob and moving into a house not dissimilar to the one I grew up in. No longer feeling the pressure to conform, to be the perfect doctor's wife. I started to allow bits of the old Alice back. And I liked it. I liked me. And then I realised: Rob had liked me too. The old Alice, I mean. So it seems only fair I give both of us a chance to let her back into our lives.'

Serena sat back in the booth and smoothed her wild curls. 'Alice, it all makes perfect sense,' she told her friend. 'And I so hope it all works out for you. I really do.'

'Thank you,' Alice said. 'So do I . . . But enough about me. I want a proper low-down on everything to do with getting Winter back. Oh, Serena,' she said, 'it really has ended so perfectly for you.'

39.
NOVEMBER 2015

The following night was a rare evening alone for Serena. Well, not entirely alone. Winter was asleep in her cot and Paddington was guarding the nursery door, mistakenly believing her role in life was to be a guard cat to the rowdy newcomer. Daft, but rather sweet. Will was visiting Miss Dawson, who'd received bad news about a relative. It wasn't great timing for Will, who just wanted to be with his new family at the moment, but Miss Dawson had seemed unusually vulnerable when she'd called. Will knew that, despite her outward attitude, she was a lonely old thing and as fragile as any other human being beneath the tough exterior. Pete, meanwhile, was having supper up the road with the Colonel and Jake Hardy, while Ashna and Max had just headed to the pub for the evening.

Serena checked on Winter again, then made her way down the grand staircase. She could hear thunder: a storm rolling in, then a sudden clatter of vicious rain on the windowpanes. A momentary flash of lightning threw the hall into sudden brightness, making it look flood-lit.

Serena turned on lights, then threw another log into the wood burner in the hall. She was going to spend the evening making plans for the christening, but was distracted by the sight of the piano and realised she hadn't played since the Harvest Supper. She sat down at the stool and let her fingers brush the cool ivory keys. Then she began. A few scales to warm up, then a couple of her favourites, including Beethoven's 'Moonlight Sonata'.

It was halfway through Rachmaninov's Sonata No. 1 that it happened. She was playing, oblivious, her eyes closed as she moved to the dramatic music, which seemed to merge with the claps of thunder that boomed out louder and louder until the storm was overhead. She had no idea it was coming. All at once, she felt herself being catapulted forward, whacking her head on the piano.

'What the . . . ?' she exclaimed, jumping up, her heart pounding as she turned to face her assailant. Her forehead was throbbing, but she was too afraid to feel the pain.

Luna. There, right in front of her and soaked to the bone – her hair bedraggled and her eyes wild. Not safely incarcerated in a psychiatric unit in Inverness but at the Vicarage, where Serena and Winter were all alone.

'Where's my baby?' Luna asked, her eyes glittering dangerously.

'She's not yours. You know that. How did you find us?' asked Serena, shaking. But Luna didn't stop to answer. She was off up the stairs, quick as a flash, Serena blundering after her.

'Stop!' Serena shouted, as Luna dashed in and out of bedrooms until, finally, hearing a sleepy cry, she shoved Serena out of the way and pushed open the door of the nursery. She stood still then, quietly watching the baby stir. Another flash of lightning.

'You have to leave!' Serena whispered in agitation. 'Will's going to be home any minute.' She was panicking and in truth she had no idea when he'd be home. Luna ignored her. She looked the same as she always had, but there was something about her that was different from when Serena had last set eyes on her. Something raw, and quite unbelievably frightening.

'I'm not leaving without my baby,' Luna whispered back, her eyes gleaming in the half-light of the room.

'She's not yours.'

'*I'm* the one who carried her, gave birth to her, cared for her, fed her, got up for her through the night for ten months of her life . . .'

'And *I'm* the one who should have been doing those things. Luna, don't you see? Don't you see what a terrible thing you did? We trusted you and you stole our baby. You've always tried to take everything that's mine, but you're not having her. You're not having Winter!' Serena shouted now, her mother's instinct in full force, not caring any longer if she woke the baby.

They didn't hesitate. They both lunged for the cot, but Luna was stronger. Serena felt like she was falling in slow motion. She watched as Ashna appeared from nowhere to grab Winter, before the back of her head hit the nursery floor with a loud thump. Then, just darkness.

40.
NOVEMBER 2015

Serena awoke from a deep, groggy sleep. Her eyes felt sticky but she managed to open them, wondering where she was. A hospital bed, she realised. She spotted Will to her left, asleep in the chair beside her then felt a pressure on her hand and looked gingerly to her right.

'Thank you,' she croaked at the woman by her side, the words seeming so inadequate.

'You know what my name means?' came the reply. Serena shook her head. Her whole skull throbbed.

'Ashna means "friend" in Sanskrit. You've been such a friend to me, from the very first moment I met you. Now, finally, I feel I've repaid some of that friendship to you,' her rescuer explained.

Serena smiled weakly and shut her eyes as she felt the fog descend again. She'd always believed blood was thicker than water, but now she knew that wasn't true.

❦

By the following morning, Serena was well enough to sit up in bed with a cup of tea.

'Ouch!' she exclaimed as she leaned her head back. It was wrapped in the sort of comical bandage she'd only seen before in cartoons and soap operas.

'Grade 2 concussion,' said Will, stroking her hand. 'But thankfully you're okay. You whacked the back of your head when you fell, but you're going to be fine.'

'And Winnie?' asked Serena. 'I saw Ashna come and grab her, just as I was falling. I felt a moment of relief and then just darkness.'

'Winnie's fine, thank heavens. Ashna bumped into a lady in the pub she'd made a scarf for. Said she'd dash back to the house and grab it and, of course, when she did, she heard you shouting. She rushed upstairs and just grabbed Winnie, ran to the pub to get Max and he legged it back to the house. Max's medical training came in pretty useful – he knew exactly what to do – and he called an ambulance and the police. There was no sign of Luna, but the police have tracked her down now.'

'Where is she?'

'Being interviewed at the police station, but they're getting a mental health team involved as well.'

'Is she okay?' Serena asked and Will raised his eyes to heaven, marvelling at her ability to think of others, even now. 'I know we'll never be able to have a relationship again. But I don't wish her any harm, Will. She's my sister, after all.'

'She'll be looked after,' Will told her, hugging her to him. 'She'll be okay. And, more importantly, she won't be coming near us or Winter again. The police have assured me of that.'

A nurse popped her head around the door. 'Doctor says you can leave tomorrow afternoon,' she smiled. 'You'll be able to get back to your baby then.'

'Who's looking after her?' Serena asked Will.

'Ashna,' Will said. 'Max and Pete were her bodyguards last night while Ashna and I stayed with you, but she went back this morning to help them out. They weren't that keen on the nappy-changing! I'll take over tonight and by tomorrow this whole episode will all be over and you'll be home for Winter. She's missing you.'

∽

The following evening, Serena and Will arrived home just in time to give Winter her bath and enjoy a cosy bedtime story, before putting her to bed. The doorbell rang so Will headed downstairs while Serena sang Winter's ritual bedtime song; it was a lullaby her mother had sung to her – it had been forgotten for years, but had come to her out of the blue one evening.

Go to sleep, my sweetheart,
You're a little dear,
You're the sweetest darling
Mummy's ever been near.
Have a lovely sweet dream,
All the whole night through.
And in the morning you will see that
Mummy still loves you.

Serena kissed Winter's forehead, inhaling her gorgeous baby smell, and crept out of the nursery. She headed downstairs and, hearing conversation in the hallway, wondered who the visitor might be. She saw the back of a man, tall and white-haired.

'Hello!' she said.

'Ah, there you are!' bellowed the Colonel. He was standing next to the log burner with Will. 'Will was just telling me about the dramas you've been having. Sounds like you've been in the wars. Looks like it too. How are you, my dear?'

'Bit of a headache,' Serena admitted. 'But much, much better now I'm home again. Would you like a drink?'

The Colonel looked as though he'd like one very much, but he shook his head ruefully. 'Can't stop long, I'm afraid. Jake's waiting for me out in the Land Rover. Was just explaining to Will. I've done that research you wanted me to do. I've got some papers for you. Turns out there were at least two families who had healthy babies that grew up in the Vicarage. One in the 1920s and another in the late '50s. Seems the story about the curse was just a local myth after all,' he said, his eyes twinkling behind his wonky spectacles. He handed an A4-sized envelope to Serena. 'Now, I'd best be off!' he said, with a wave. 'See you anon!'

After thanking the Colonel and seeing him on his way, Serena, clutching the papers, looked at Will. She raised an eyebrow.

'I'm not going to say anything,' grinned Will. 'I am *definitely*, *definitely* not going to say I told you so.'

Serena laughed and thumped him on the arm.

41.
22ND DECEMBER 2015

It was the day before various out-of-town guests were due to arrive for the christening, with a view to staying on over the Christmas period. Serena and Ashna were planning to make up all the beds later in the morning and fill each room with fresh towels, flowers and brand-new squares of soap. But it was still only ten o'clock and Serena found herself unexpectedly alone in the kitchen. Winter was having her morning nap, Will and Pete were collecting the Christmas tree and Ashna was wrapping presents in her room.

The post had just arrived. A bundle of Christmas cards. Serena made herself a cup of tea and sat at the kitchen table to read them at leisure. She put her reading glasses on and sifted through them, then almost dropped the lot as she came across an envelope in her sister's distinctive hand. She put the cards to one side and slit open the envelope with a paper knife. There was a wad of pages within. She unfolded them. She took a deep breath and began to read.

'*Dear Serena,*' the letter began. '*It's almost Christmas and I'm about to "enjoy" a carol service being held at the mental health unit (a.k.a. loony bin!). I truly hope I'm not expected to sing: you know what my voice is like. I never could hold a note! There are at least two men in here who think they're Jesus so I'm wondering whether they think*

Christmas Day is their birthday and will each expect a cake generously decorated with candles. I shall soon find out.

I'm being too flippant and familiar, aren't I? Such behaviour tends to indicate a distinct lack of remorse. I'm learning all these subtleties in my therapy sessions. The psychotherapist is called Sean and he reminds me of Uncle Clive: flyaway white hair that he tries to sweep over an enormous bald patch in the hope no one will notice the polished egg beneath (tricky in windy weather!). He wears a "zany" bow tie and has a paunch on which he rests his effeminate hands. He's okay though. Talks a lot of sense, actually. He suggested I write to you to explain. So here I go . . .

I didn't ever set out to steal Winter. Ever since I did the dirty on you with Freddie, I've tried to be a better person. Ironically, offering to be your surrogate was part of my "be nicer" campaign. It was at the twelve-week scan that I felt the first flutterings of maternal instinct. I tried not to look at the screen, but just before the sonographer turned it off I snuck a glance. I saw a little baby there, clear as day. I ignored the instinct for as long as I could. But when I started to feel the baby dancing around in my tummy, there was no denying it. I'd started to fall in love.

I couldn't tell you. Of course I couldn't. But I began to realise I would never be able to hand the baby over to you. I felt terrible as I made my plans to run away. I knew what I was doing would be torture for you, and an even worse betrayal than the last one. But I told myself that you, at least, had Will. Without the baby, I had no one. I reached the peak of self-disgust on the day of the twenty-week scan. First I lied and told you the baby was a boy so I'd be harder to track down, and then we went shopping and you were so happy and excited, dashing in and out of stores buying masses of pale blue toys and outfits. I hated myself. And yet . . .

I left. I wasn't going to leave until I was nearer to the due date, but after our shopping trip I knew I couldn't stick around and watch your growing anticipation any longer. I had it all worked out: I'd been saving money for a while and I'd managed to locate and rent a little bothy in the wilds of Scotland. I'd had everything I'd need for the birth and the baby's needs delivered in advance, so we wouldn't need to see another soul.

I'll spare you the gory details about the birth, but we managed. I know now I put the baby at risk doing it with just a local farmer's wife to help me and – above all else – I'm sorry for that.

Those weeks with a newborn were very special but, I must admit, also pretty tough. I felt lonely more than anything. Well, lonely and guilty. Whenever I looked into Winter's blue eyes, I saw Will. They were like a reproach. We only set foot outside the bothy once after she was born, to register her birth, and it was so stressful I swore I wouldn't leave the place again.

I couldn't stand the loneliness in the end. I contacted Seb. He came to stay – I told him a fib about escaping a violent boyfriend – and we restarted a relationship. It was lovely, but I knew it all had a sell-by date. I felt, as time passed, that the walls were closing in on me. That's when I started to self-harm again. A release, I suppose.

I think you know everything that happened after that. I went crazy when Mum and Seb took Winter. I spent the first few days sedated in the Scottish madhouse. Then, one day, I didn't take the medication. I escaped and hitched lifts all the way to Sussex. As you know, I wasn't in a good state. I would have done anything right then to get Winter back. I hurt you, physically, on top of all the mental anguish I'd caused. I'm so sorry. I'm a terrible sister: I always have been.

I know we'll never have a relationship again and that, in trying to keep Winter, I've robbed myself of the chance of even being a doting auntie. I'm alone now and I'm fairly sure I'll stay that way. I'm getting treatment though, and I'm starting to address this ruthlessness that seems to run through me like the writing in a stick of rock. Perhaps one day I'll be cured.

I'm not sure yet whether I'm going to be prosecuted but I know you told the police you don't want to press charges, which just goes to show what a generous person you are.

I expect nothing of you at all. Of course I don't. No forgiveness. No further contact. I ask of you only one thing. Please tell Winter I love her. And that I always will.

Your mad and sorry sister,

Luna xxx'

Serena put the letter down on the table, tears streaming down her face. Luna would never be a part of her life again, but she was so grateful for the letter. It gave her closure. She went over to the dresser and rummaged around in the cupboard, at last finding what she was searching for: a framed photograph of Luna that had never seen the light of day since they'd been living at the Vicarage in Cattlebridge.

She heard a cry on the baby monitor. Winter was awake. She hurried upstairs.

'Hello, darling,' she said, finding Winter playing with her bunny in the cot. Serena opened the blind, then picked the baby up and carried her over to the mantelpiece where she carefully positioned the framed photograph. A momentary ray of sunshine glinted on the glass.

'Auntie Luna,' she said to Winter, and the baby reached a hand towards the photo. She looked at it and smiled.

42.
23RD DECEMBER 2015

The day before the christening was a frenzy of excitement. Stephanie and Brian arrived, laden with luggage and an abundance of gifts for Winter. Then Bernie Pemberton and his new wife, Betty, needed picking up from the station, having taken the train all the way from South Devon.

Bernie was a newly retired vicar and a very old friend of Will's father – the very person who'd inspired Will to become a vicar himself. So when Will's own parents told him that sadly they wouldn't be able to make the christening due to his father's poor health, Will and Serena had decided to invite Bernie and Betty in loco parentis. Happily, Bernie's younger daughter, Rosamunde, who'd been due to spend Christmas with Bernie and Betty, had agreed to join the party in East Sussex.

It was particularly accommodating of Rosamunde, as she was heavily pregnant with her first child and her boyfriend was spending a few days with his family before joining the rest of the group in Sussex on Christmas Eve. This meant that Rosamunde had driven all the way on her own, with a dog in the back of the car. He instantly made himself at home by the log burner in the hall with Max's dogs, Basil and Manuel, and Paddington decided to treat him with the same disdain she felt towards the Labradors. The dog sighed with resignation. He was used to such treatment from cats.

Serena's friend Lisa and her family had arrived in the village as well, with plans to visit Lisa's family after the christening, although they were staying with Alice and Rob at the Georgian house for a couple of nights (Alice having just moved back in). Both Lisa and Alice were going to be godmothers, as well as Ashna.

Having settled her own house guests in their rooms to recover from their journeys, Serena set about transforming the dining room with Ashna's help – it was the only place with a large enough table to seat so many guests for dinner. They polished the table, hung fairy lights over picture frames, pulled Ashna's floral curtains against the dark evening and lit thick, cream church candles, which flickered cosily.

Winter had been bathed and snuggled up in her cot and then, after a number of guests had made their own use of the now constant supply of hot water, everyone congregated in the little-used drawing room for pre-dinner drinks, each of them looking and smelling delicious.

'Well, don't you all look gimsy,' Mrs Pipe told them unsmilingly, after delivering the drinks. She left the room.

'She means smart,' Serena translated. She was becoming quite a dab hand at old Sussex provincialisms.

The drawing-room fire was crackling away and an enormous Christmas tree, decorated haphazardly by the household the evening before, had been installed in the corner, its lights twinkling.

A festive dinner ensued, with Mrs Pipe helping to serve and clear the plates. An enormous ham served with new potatoes and asparagus, followed by a lemon cheesecake: Will's speciality. As well as the guests who'd travelled from afar, all of the Vicarage residents were in attendance, including Max, who stayed there most of the time now. The main course finished, he cleared his throat and asked for a moment. Everyone stopped chatting and looked at him.

'I'm sorry to interrupt,' he said, 'but I just wanted to tell you. We're so excited. Ashna and I are engaged. I proposed to her this morning! Down at the beach in Camber.'

There were gasps of delight and details were provided, Max explaining that the first practical step to be taken would be a divorce for him, as he was still technically married to the vile Lara.

'That could take a little while, so I'm going to move in with Max after Christmas and we'll slowly start making plans,' Ashna told them all, looking flushed and happy. She held out her hand so her engagement ring could be admired.

Once all the excitement and chatter over this news had died down, Serena turned back to Rosamunde.

'So, only two weeks to go until the due date,' Serena said. Rosamunde had beautiful long red hair and an enormous bump, and looked utterly radiant in the glow of candlelight. She seemed peaceful and content.

'It's crept up on me all of a sudden,' Rosamunde replied. 'I've brought my hospital bag with me, just in case!' She had joked then, although a few hours later, in the grips of labour pains, she was no longer laughing.

❧

At two o'clock in the morning, Rosamunde knocked on the door of the master bedroom.

'Come in!' called Serena, switching on the dim little bedside light. Will was asleep, but when Serena saw Rosamunde at the door she gave him a dig in the ribs and he sat up blearily. 'Is everything okay?' asked Serena.

'I think I'm in labour,' Rosamunde gasped. 'I know they say you should relax at home rather than going into hospital too soon, but my contractions seem to be quite strong and regular so I think I'd rather get there. I'm sorry to wake you, but I don't know how to get to the hospital.'

'I'll take you,' said Will, immediately hopping out of bed. 'I only had one glass of wine with dinner – most unlike me! Don't worry – it'll only take twenty minutes at this time of night.'

Serena wrapped herself in a dressing gown and, while Will got dressed, she helped Rosamunde back to the guest bedroom she was occupying.

'Rosamunde, I'm so excited for you!' she whispered. 'But what about your boyfriend?'

'He's on his way.' Rosamunde gripped Serena's arm, in the throes of a contraction. 'It's a long drive, but hopefully he'll make it.'

Rosamunde had managed to dress in leggings and a diaphanous tunic top and she now started to hurl items she'd unpacked for her stay into her hospital bag. She stopped for a moment and her face contorted with agony again. She bent over the bed. Serena moved towards her.

'Shall I rub your back?' she asked.

'Please,' Rosamunde whispered. After a short time, her face and body relaxed again. She turned towards Serena.

'Serena, I'm terrified,' she said, rubbing her belly. 'What if I can't do it? Or something goes wrong? I'm an ancient mother: I'm forty-five! Maybe I'm too old to do this . . .'

'Age has got nothing to do with it,' Serena told her, gripping her hand. 'You look miles younger. It's just a question of attitude, like anything in life. You'll manage. Of course you will. And once you get to the hospital, you'll be in the best hands. My friend Alice's husband might even deliver the baby. He's an obstetrician. You'll be able to have some pain relief as well, once you get there. That'll help. Now, have you got everything?'

'I think so. Serena, would you be able to let my dad and Betty know I've gone to the hospital when you see them in the morning? I don't want to wake them now.'

'Of course!'

Will arrived in the doorway. 'Ready?' he asked.

'Yep. Hang on!' Rosamunde groaned through another contraction. As soon as it stopped, Will seized his chance.

'Quick, let's get you in the car now before the next one. Bye, Serena! See you later. I'll keep you posted!' He hurried out, one arm around Rosamunde, the other grasping the hospital bag and pregnancy notes.

Serena followed them, on her way back to her room, and it occurred to her that Will was finally getting to enjoy that exciting rite of passage of taking a heavily pregnant woman to hospital for the birth of a child. She felt a little wistful for a moment.

At the top of the stairs, Rosamunde stopped and turned her head. 'Thank you,' she said to Serena. 'You've made me feel so much better.'

Serena blew her a kiss. 'Good luck!' she called out and as they left, she said a little prayer.

43.
CHRISTMAS EVE 2015

It was Christmas Eve. Serena's favourite day of the season, made all the more special by it being Winter's birthday (Will had managed to find out from the Scottish birth registry that, amazingly, Winter had been born on her due date). Serena was waiting for Will to get back from the hospital before giving Winter her presents. She checked her watch as she cleared the breakfast table and saw it was nearly nine. Five minutes later, Will came pounding down the stairs to the kitchen.

'Any news?' Serena asked immediately.

'No, but she's well and truly in the thick of it. Her boyfriend arrived half an hour ago, so she released me. She wouldn't let me go when I got to the hospital with her. I'm sure I was fairly useless, but she said she wanted a familiar face. The midwives were a bit confused. We had to keep explaining we weren't a couple!'

Serena laughed. 'How was she doing? Was it agony?'

'Horrendous. I had no idea these things go on for so long either. They were talking about an epidural when I left, so she might get a bit of rest before the pushing bit starts. Goodness, it made me very glad to be a man.'

'You'll think I'm mad but, even though it sounds awful, I'd still have loved to experience it.'

Will put his arms out and embraced her. 'I know,' he said into her hair. Serena took a deep breath and looked up at him.

'You look exhausted,' she said. 'Why don't you go and have a bath and a nap and we'll do Winnie's presents just before lunch?'

'That sounds like heaven. I'll go and run a bath now. You couldn't bring me up a cup of tea, could you?'

'Will do,' Serena promised. 'And some toast. But you'd better just quickly pop your head round Bernie's door and update him and Betty on how Rosamunde's doing. They're so excited!'

As planned, everyone in the house congregated for Winter's present-opening ceremony just before lunch. She thoroughly enjoyed being the star of the show, soon getting the hang of ripping open the wrapping paper on all her presents. The attention didn't stop there either, as it was also the day of Winter's christening.

The service was due to start at five o'clock so that it could take place in candlelight and an open invitation had been given to all the parishioners to attend the service and enjoy some mulled wine at the back of the church afterwards, although just family and close friends would head back to the Vicarage for the after-party.

Serena felt she was becoming quite a pro at catering for groups and parties now, with Mrs Pipe's help. It was now nearly four o'clock and she had just taken a batch of mince pies out of the oven while Ashna fed Winter her tea. The baby was smothered in yogurt and would need a good clean-up before being buttoned into the precious family christening robe.

'Brandy butter!' Serena exclaimed. 'I knew I'd forgotten some-thing. Are you happy to carry on feeding Winnie while I run to the shops? It's early closing today so I'd better go now.'

'Of course, don't rush. I'll give her a quick bath and start get-ting her into her gown once we're done,' replied Ashna, and Serena gave both of them a kiss before dashing upstairs, where Mrs Pipe chased after her with her parka.

'Don't ye forget this,' she said, 'it's winter-proud out there, it is.' Serena took the coat gratefully. She dashed along the lane to the high street, discovering Mrs Pipe was right. It was freezing, with ominous dark clouds low in the sky.

She ran into the grocer's and picked up some brandy butter, as well as a couple of other items (impossible to have too much milk), then began to hurry back towards the Vicarage. But then, suddenly, she slowed down, realising it was her favourite time of day on her favourite day of the year. She wanted to enjoy it. Dusk, and no one had yet pulled their curtains, allowing Serena to observe scenes of such utter cosiness she felt as though she were watching a Richard Curtis film.

Nearly every window of every cottage along the high street seemed to showcase a festive scene within, with Christmas trees of all different shapes and sizes, bedecked with decorations and lights, presents scattered around the base. Some trees were taste-fully arranged, with gleaming white lights, while others were more of a mishmash of childishly made treasures and bright and garish illuminations.

And then, of course, each house had a fire – some in inglenooks or tiny hearths, while others had log burners or gas fires – all roaring away, keeping the cold at bay and lending a sense of festive comfort to each house.

Behind one window was an elderly gentleman dozing in an armchair while an unwatched television flickered brightly in the corner. In another, a black-and-white cat was sitting on the windowsill, beside a nativity set, scrutinising Serena as she paused for a moment to look inside. In the next house, a young mother read to her child on the sofa, the little boy with his thumb firmly in his mouth, his head leaning on her shoulder. A few doors along, a couple laughed as they wrapped presents together, kneeling on the hearthrug. The woman looked up and spotted Serena. She smiled, but quickly got up and drew the curtains across.

Enough. It was time to retreat to her own home – to the Vicarage and the joys that were awaiting her there. Joys that Serena had thought until recently she would never know.

The house was, she now realised, the very opposite of cursed. It was lucky.

EPILOGUE
CHRISTMAS EVE 2015

On the way to the church, it began to snow. Gentle tickly flakes that settled in everyone's hair, making them look as though they had bad dandruff.

'About time too,' said Will. 'They've been promising us snow for days. Wish I'd put a bet on a white Christmas.'

'I did,' twinkled Pete, smiling smugly.

When they arrived at the door, Will spotted a lady he'd never met before, timidly entering the church.

'You must be Shilpa!' said Will, introducing himself to a petite, middle-aged woman. 'Let me take you to Ashna. She'll be so pleased you could make it. You will join us later, won't you?'

Ashna, on spotting her mother, ran over and embraced her with such emotion that Will felt a lump rise in his throat. He left them to enjoy their reunion.

The service that ensued was magical. The church was packed – even Paddington turned up, wondering where Winter, her charge, had got to. The pews were bathed in candlelight, meaning everyone had to squint to read the service sheets, but nobody seemed to mind. They joined in heartily with various carols and when Winter was taken up to the font for the christening, all the little children in the church were invited to come to the front to be able to see more clearly and to join in with a tenderly sung 'Away in a Manger'.

Will was in charge for most of the service but Bernie took over for the actual baptism, meaning Will could play a proper fatherly role in the proceedings.

'Now, could the godparents all stand over here,' instructed Bernie. 'That's right, mind yourselves, we don't want any of you catching fire.' There was a titter amongst the congregation and the godparents – Max, Pete, Ashna, Alice and Lisa – took their positions and replied solemnly as Bernie took them through the necessary questions.

Then Bernie took hold of little Winter and there was hardly a dry eye in the church as he baptised her.

He dipped her slightly into the font and made the sign of the cross on her forehead with the holy water.

'Winter Ashna Blacksmith, I baptise you in the name of the Father, and of the Son, and of the Holy Spirit. Amen. Good girl, I knew you wouldn't cry,' Bernie said as Winter looked at him, baffled. He lit a candle, which seemed to mesmerise the baby, then he asked: 'Mind if I do the rounds with her?' Will and Serena shook their heads.

'Here we go,' said Bernie, as he carried Winter in his large and capable arms down the aisle and back again. She beamed at her admirers and even started waving – a rather regal wave that made everyone laugh.

'Phew!' Bernie said, handing her back to Will. 'Always a relief when you manage not to drop them, isn't it?' He smiled and stroked Winter's fluffy head, before Will handed the baby to Serena and took over the last part of the service.

They were about to sing one last carol when there was a loud crash as the church door swung open and shut. A man bumbled in, his eyes bright and his cheeks pink. He made his way to a pew, tripping over a hassock. Every head in the church turned to look. Will recognised him as Rosamunde's boyfriend: they'd met briefly at the hospital earlier in the day.

'Has she had the baby?' Will called out, unable to help himself.

The chap stood up, looking embarrassed yet ecstatic. 'Yes!' he called back. 'A great big baby boy. Buster William. We're going to call him Buster Bill. He's amazing and Rosamunde's fine. Tired, but very happy.'

'Fantastic news!' replied Will and he started to clap, the entire congregation joining in even though they didn't have a clue who this man was. Betty Pemberton even wolf-whistled, causing Miss Dawson to frown and purse her lips. She'd fully recovered from the fleeting *joie de vivre* that had transformed her on the night of the Harvest Supper.

'And now, our final carol – "Silent Night",' Will said when the applause had died down.

The carol sung, the service almost finished, Will delivered his final blessing, before advising everyone about the mulled wine available at the back of the church.

'One last thing,' Will said. 'I want to thank you all so much for coming to Winter's christening today. It means the world to us to feel so welcomed into the village.'

'About time too,' piped up the Colonel. 'And may I ask you a question on behalf of your parishioners?'

'Of course,' said Will, raising his eyebrows enquiringly.

'Well, now that your lovely baby's been christened, can we expect to hear wedding bells anytime soon?'

Will glanced at Serena. She gave a very gentle nod, almost imperceptible to anyone but him.

'Maybe,' Will said with a smile. 'Just maybe . . .'

AUTHOR'S NOTE AND ACKNOWLEDGEMENTS

I remember starting to write my first novel on holiday in Menorca at the age of nine and a gust of wind blowing the pages into the swimming pool. Not a good start! But all these years later, I'm thrilled to have written my second novel and I certainly couldn't have done it (nor, indeed, my first book) without the support and encouragement of these wonderful people: my amazing husband, Dan (for everything, not least the amusing first edit!); my beautiful girls – Ruby Hope and Iris Rose; my mum, Lorna (who was once a young vicar's wife living in a haunted Vicarage); my late father, Reverend John Lambourne (whose younger self I tried to capture in Will); my siblings – Matt (stories of Dad), Kate (medical facts checker) and Vix (all-round supporter) – and their families; my late grandparents; Sarah Lambourne and my twin nieces, Jenn and Rach, for help with the twin research (neither twin is remotely like Luna, I hasten to add!); my uncle, aunts and cousins; Sarah and Graham Boxall; my sibs-in-law – Sophs, Har and Jess – and their families (thanks, Pete, for the Aussie lingo and beer expertise!); Fox Force Five (Nats, Emma, Toni and Amanda); Ruth Faye; Elizabeth Kilgarriff; Beth Say; Mini Book Club (including Becky Jury); Kate and Jason Mills; Damian James and Kate Motley; Pat and Bianca O'Connor;

my old mate Martin and his sister, Helen Alkin; the godfathers (Chris and Chris); the Pilcher family; my wonderful childminder, Ali Lewis; Gillian Smith of Belle Flowers in Robertsbridge; Geoffrey Whitehead; Bex M, Holly and Lilli; Liz Sheehan; Rachel (creative writing classes!); and – last but not least – the fabulous MLA team (Jo Stafford-Power, Grieveous, Sue and Mr B). As well, I must thank all the reviewers and kind people who have contacted me with positive feedback in relation to my first book and expressed interest in a second. Finally, my thanks go to Amazon Publishing, including Sammia Hamer, Sophie Missing, Monica Byles, Ian Critchley and the rest of the incredibly lovely and hard-working team (and to Jodi Warshaw and Emilie Marneur for finding me in the first place!).

This book is in memory of my maternal grandfather's aunt, Connie, who made the most exquisite christening gown when her sister was expecting him, but sadly died at the age of twenty-one before he was born. It always struck me as such a sad story. The gown has since been worn by thirty babies in my family.

BIBLIOGRAPHY

Reverend W. D. Parish, *A Dictionary of the Sussex Dialect*, intro-
duced by Lynne Truss (Snake River Press, 2008).
Robin Guild, *The Victorian House Book: A Practical Guide to Home
Repair and Decoration* (Sheldrake Press, 4th edition, 2007).

ABOUT THE AUTHOR

Rebecca Boxall was born in 1977 in East Sussex, where she grew up in a bustling vicarage always filled with family, friends and parishioners. She now lives by the sea in Jersey with her husband and two children. She read English at the University of Warwick before training as a lawyer and also studied Creative Writing with The Writers Bureau. *Home for Winter* is her second novel.

Printed in Great Britain
by Amazon